The Islands

DRUE HEINZ LITERATURE PRIZE

The Islands

SIX FICTIONS

William Wall

University of Pittsburgh Press

Published by the University of Pittsburgh Press, Pittsburgh, PA, 15260
Copyright © 2017, William Wall
All rights reserved
Manufactured in the United States of America
Printed on acid-free paper
10 9 8 7 6 5 4 3 2 1

Cataloging-in-Publication data is available from the Library of Congress

ISBN 13: 978-0-8229-4519-2
ISBN 10: 0-8229-4519-3

Jacket design by Regina Starace

For Liz

Amor, ch'a nullo amato amar perdona . . .

Love, which never absolves a loved one from loving . . .

DANTE, Inferno

CONTENTS

The Islands

GRACE'S DAY

Grace

A long time ago I had two sisters and we lived on an island. There was me and Jeannie and Em. They called me Grace, but I have never had much of that. I was an awkward child. I still am all these years later. Our house had two doors, one to the south, one to the north. Its garden looked towards the setting sun. It was a garden of apple trees and fuchsia and everything in it leaned away from the wind. Dry stone walls encircled it and sheep and children broke them down. My mother lived there with us. Boats came and went bringing food and sometimes sheep, and there were times when we lived by catching fish and rabbits, though we were not so good at either. Richard Wood came in the *Iliad*, his wooden yawl, always it seemed when a gale of wind threatened. He dropped his anchor in the sound and stayed for nights at a time. Mother said he liked his home comforts. He was younger than her, though not by much, and she was younger than Father. Father liked to come first, she said. In summertime we swam naked in the crystal water and saw his anchor bedded in the sand, the marks the chain left where it swung to tide or wind. Many a time I swam down that chain, hauling myself deeper, hand over hand, until I could stand on the bottom. But he took no notice. In calm weather we could see my footprints on the seabed as if I lived down there and had stood a long time in one place looking up. Or perhaps that was not how it happened. Words have that way of invading memory; the stories they tell us become our stories. What I remember and what I forget may be one and the same thing, or they may merely depend upon each other. And what my father remembered for me.

There were three islands and they were youth, childhood, and age, and I searched for my father in every one.

Jeannie

My first memory, the first memory that I can certainly say wasn't given to me by someone else is of my father hoisting me onto his shoulders so that I could see something. What do you see, Jeannie, he says, what do you see? We're in a crowd and my mother Jane is there. I don't remember whether my sister Grace is there or not and I don't know what it is that I want to see. It must have been before Em was born. What I remember most clearly is the enormous sense of safety and sureness coupled with a giddy vertigo. I remember looking down on the crowd. Many men wear cloth caps and the women wear scarves, as they did still in those days, and my father is smoking a pipe and I can smell the tobacco. One man turns and says something like, What you think of that then, Tom? And Tom takes the pipe from his mouth, releasing my leg in the process, and says something I don't catch. Even now it only takes someone lighting a pipe outside a restaurant for a great wave of security to possess me. Tom is not a tall man but from the height of his shoulders everyone around looks small. Hold on, Jeannie, he says to me, and swings round and moves through the crowd and out onto the street and there I see a horse; a man is holding him by the bridle, and I remember steam coming off his back and steam coming from a large greenish-brown shit on the road behind him. I can smell the horse and he smells like Tom's old coat.

All my early memories of him are like that. Shelter, comfort, pleasant smells and sounds. I hear his voice sometimes—in the street or in a park or in a quiet room—and I turn expecting to see him. My expectation is always of a young man, trim, loose-limbed, fine-boned, coming towards me in his tweed jacket with something in his hand. My father the gift bringer, bearer of news, the world traveler bringing stones from Italy, California, India. I was a collector of stones. I was his favorite. I make no apologies. I loved him the most. Grace, on the other hand, could never love anyone or anything without some reserve of herself; she has a kind of native hostility or cynicism that prevents her from ever being wholeheartedly loving towards anybody. She's one of those people who feels the world has cheated her of some special experience. I pity her for that.

Grace

One day on our island my sister Jeannie ran in to say that
she had seen a whale in the sound and I ran out after her, my
mother calling me: Grace, it's your day, take Em. But I was too
excited. And there were three fin whales making their way into
the rising tide. We heard their breathing. It carried perfectly in
the still grey air. It was reflected back at us by the low cloud. The
sea was still and burnished. We ran along the rocks watching for
their breaching. We decided it was a mother, a father, and a calf.
They were in no hurry. When we reached the beacon, a small
unlit concrete marker indicating the western end of the island,
we watched them breaching and diving into the distance until we
could see them no more. But they left behind their calmness and
the unhurried but forceful sound of their blows. We were wearing
our summer shorts, and so, once the whales were no longer to be
seen, I pulled mine off, threw Jeannie my shirt, and plunged in
and swam out into the rising tide and allowed myself to be carried
along outside everything and back to the anchorage. That was
how, so far out, drifting like a seal in the tide, I saw my mother
kissing Richard Wood against the gable of our house. It did not
come as a shock or a surprise but I felt a sickening sense of guilt

and shame and I allowed myself to be carried past the anchored yawl and too far out into the sound, so that it was a struggle and a hard swim to get back. My sisters, Jeannie and Em, watched me sullenly for a long time. I think if I had drowned they would have watched that too with the same sullen disinterest. When I came ashore I was exhausted. I threw myself down on the strand and lay staring at the clouds for a long time. My mother was wearing her slacks and a jumper. Her sleeves were rolled back. She had put on weight and I could clearly see the bulge of her stomach low down, pressed against his belt. His hands were on her back inside the jumper. They could not have been seen from the shore. At that time my father was already in England. His name was mentioned in newspapers and from time to time when he wrote home, usually sending a check, he included clippings and reviews.

It's possible that Jeannie already hated me, because while I lay on the sand she prised a large stone out of the shale and brought it steadfastly towards me, approaching from behind, and dropped it on my chest. The shock almost stopped my breath. I think she may well have been trying to kill me, but at five or six she simply didn't have the height to do it. The stone simply didn't reach a sufficient velocity. It landed flat and made a flat sound that I heard in my body, rather than felt, and I was too stunned to cry. I feel certain she dropped it on my chest rather than my head because she wanted to stop my heart. Had she been older she would have tried for my brain instead.

By the time I had recovered my breath she was gone. I searched for her, steadily and ruthlessly working my way west through the hiding places that I knew, and found her near the old tower, crouched in the bracken. She had already forgotten why she was hiding. She had feathers and a collection of bracken fronds, playing some game that involved talking in voices. She did not hear my approach. I caught her from behind by the hair, which was shoulder length at that time, and swung her onto her back. I was on her then and we fought hard, scratching and pulling, and in the end we had each other by the hair, slapping and pinching and kicking until, rolling off me, she struck her head on a stone and began to cry. I can see her now, a pitiful, snotty-nosed waif curled in a ball, holding her head and wailing for her mother. Now I feel nothing but shame at the memory but at the time I laughed at her, because children know that laughing is the most hurtful reaction to pain, and she ran away again.

She was gone for the rest of the day and we had to search the island to bring her home for tea. By then the calm was gone and Richard Wood was talking anxiously about his anchor and declaring repeatedly that he should make a run for it, and my mother was pressing him to stay.

My father's books, and his color pieces for the *Manchester Guardian*, depicting a family surviving on an island on the edge of the world, part fiction, part memoir, were all the rage when we were children. This was the late 1960s and the world had fallen in love simultaneously with two incompatible mistresses—self-sufficiency and conspicuous consumption. The books represented the former, but my father, I would eventually discover, was more given at a personal level to the latter. It was my mother, my sisters, and I who held the responsibility of acting out the life he felt bound to follow. We were the ones who lived in what he liked to call the peasant economy.

We called it Castle Island, but there never was a castle, only a lonely watchtower, tall enough to survey the whole island and the sound and the ocean beyond, part of a network of revenue-gathering outposts, not to mention occasional piracy, sometime in the fifteenth century, and now just two walls on the side of a cliff where even the crows did not think it safe to nest. He bought the land with the advance from his first book—in those days you couldn't give land away in Ireland—and installed us in what had been the last occupied house on the eastern shore, near a sweet well, in the shadow of the apple orchard, by a sheltered anchorage and a small sandy strand. We were his experiment; he took readings of us as required. We were his instruments and his utopia.

There were fields where we tried to grow potatoes and salt-burnt kale and onions. Other things too, perhaps, that I have not remembered. We kept hens one summer and had eggs for breakfast, dinner, and tea until the time came to pack up and leave again. Then there was nothing we could do for the hens. The following spring there was no trace of them. We never repeated the experiment. We had a cat who kept the mice at bay—Flanagan was his name. He was white as snow and his eyes were like stones. When Father was there he set a fixed trotline of hooks across the mouth of the strand and in the morning he often had fish—plaice, dabs, flounder, bass. Our job was to dig the worms at low tide and hunt under rocks for ragworm, and in the evenings to thread the hooks with the worms and lay them out so that they didn't foul each other as they ran out. He took photographs. *The children baiting hooks.* We appear in more than one volume. In the morning he pulled the silver creatures ashore and we cooked plaice for breakfast and had bass for dinner. This was before the fishery had been ruined. He wrote about it all, of course: *Living an Island, Loving the World,* by Tom Newman. Now out of print.

When he was at home the house was warmer, fuller, brighter; it functioned as a home and a house, and we functioned as a family. When he went away we settled back into our animal existence. After a few weeks without him the house lost his presence. It began to be possible to think of him as a character we had read about, someone of enormous energy and vision whose part had been to bring life to the other characters, a catalyst at work among lethargic elements. But the elements only appeared lethargic. Things happened that no one has ever explained. And the dynamic by which we related was frightening and selfish and destructive. When I think of it now I realize that it was not that he made things happen, but that he prevented things from happening. And when he was away there was no god to stand in the doorway and watch inside and out, and what happened inside the house and what happened in the fields, in the orchard, and along the shore were both separate and different and inseparable and the same.

Richard Wood was a poet and my father's friend, but he was of course also my mother's and my sister Jeannie's lover. He was a beautiful man. He was tall and thin and he moved his limbs with the grace of one who was at home in several elements. We thought he understood the air and could tell from simply breathing it what tomorrow would bring. He understood the shapes of clouds and had categorized them and knew rhymes that interpreted them.

Mackerel skies and mares' tails, he would say, make lofty ships carry low sails.

Or: When the rain comes before the wind, topsail sheets and halyards mind.

It was a kind of knowledge that was useful on an island and we wanted it. I see him standing on the highest rock in the face of the marching seas and looking to windward like a god or a figure in a painting. I don't think he ever did that, but the memory is there, as real as a fact. Richard, what do you see? Is the future in the wind? Not now, my dear, not now. More than once he said to me that what landsmen think of as the smell of the sea was, to a sailor, the smell of the land and the smell of danger.

He knew the meaning of the weather systems and could tell by the frequency and length of waves how far away a new gale might be. He understood the compass and the Admiralty chart with its discrete symbolism and fine lines. He could calculate tides and knew when his keel would scrape over the bar and when it would run into the sand. He knew the changes in the seabed from mile to mile, and he knew what places would be bad on a rising tide and westerly wind, and what would be bad on an ebb or with the wind in the east. He was, in a way, a more primitive man than my father. But he was also more elegant and refined. My father had been born a Catholic, whereas Richard had been born into the last vestiges of the ascendancy class. He spoke with that standard Anglo-Irish accent. He had been to a boarding school in England where he had learned to write poetry about poor people and to ignore anyone he didn't choose to notice.

He fell in love with my mother when he heard her reading aloud to my father in the residents' lounge of a hotel. This is the story my mother told me, although when it took place, and whether it was actually for my father she was reading, and what the hotel was I never knew. Something about the way she told it years later suggested that it was an invention.

Richard had been asleep in a chair facing the window and they thought they were alone. She had taken a copy of Shelley's works from the hotel's bookshelves and was mockingly declaiming "The Masque of Anarchy." That was in the days when hotels kept a store of the classics in case their guests were at a loss for something to do; nowadays they buy their books from interior designers. He fell in love with her then, she said.

So, we grew up on an island that was, in memory and in fact, more like a film set of my father's devising than a real place. Even as we children lived it, it had a secondhand feel, a parallel untouchable reality that was more like the reality of art. But of that reality there is this to say:

It was less than half a mile long. It was shallow at its eastern end and the strange behavior of tides left sand in the long interstices of the rocks. Even on calm days there was the rumor of sea among stones, the grinding of pebbles. Between ourselves and The Calf, which was the next island in the sound, was a channel of about half a mile, ten fathoms deep at its most profound, but also containing a bar of the same sand that dried to a sheet of lead at the lowest spring tides. Seabirds met there in gabbling congregation for the cockles and so did we, Jeannie and I. The cockles were delicious. Jeannie would crack them open on a stone and eat them raw. Mother boiled them in milk.

Long ago the land had been divided by dry stone walls into fields of varying sizes. Now the couch grass was thick as a cushion everywhere, and wherever the limestone pavement came close to the surface heather had possession. The man from whom we bought our house still owned some of these fields and we let him graze ours. He brought sheep here in the spring and so we never owned a dog, although a dog might have been a friend, and might have warned us against trouble when it came.

On the height, on the cliff that faced towards the mainland, was the ruined watchtower, and in the shadow of the watchtower a cluster of ruined cottages. The ground among the cottages seemed to be always wet. There was a spring there, I think, anyway the sheep went there to drink. Under the tower was an ancient crumbling pier and slipway. There was an iron bollard and a rusted windlass. We could have recovered the windlass—it was one of my father's projects—the parts were all intact, and if we had done so we could have used the slip to haul our boat out of the way of the sea, but it was never done and instead we hauled it up on the sand at high water and carried the anchor up into the grass. Sometimes we swam here, but I was the only one who would jump from the pier. At high tide the drop was ten feet but at the bottom of the

ebb it was almost thirty. The water was deep, in any case, and I
was always the fearless one. I belonged to the sea as much as the
land. My mother said I was one of the sea people and the seals
were my cousins. And I believed her. They loved my grey-green
eyes and I loved their slow cool appraisal of everything. Whenever
I saw one I wanted to take my clothes off and follow. I imagined
an inverted life where the wave was my sky, an underwater world
of the underside of boats and islands and the mountains of the
continental shelf.

Gales came and went, of course, because our home was a tiny
island in the face of the Atlantic. Seas came to us from other continents. A fetch of a thousand miles is nothing to a storm. There
were nights when it seemed the universe was conspiring to drown
us all, the air and rain falling on our house as though we lived
inside a tin drum. Later, when daylight came, we would look to
see if apple trees had come down, if there was seaweed in the
branches, blisters of salt spume, if the ditches were littered with
things from the water. The sea boiled over the rocks consuming
and retiring, consuming and retiring, bright green and white and
iron grey, the surface, as far as the grey uncertain horizon, fretted,
broken, chaotic. Those were the days I loved.

But once I remember a yacht going by, water streaming over
its leeward deck, hard pressed in a sudden gale, and one of the
crew had a long handline out—it was the mackerel season. But
they had caught a seagull, or more likely the seagull caught the
hook, as happens when the line is towed too fast and the lead hops
from wave to wave. And they were towing the terrified bird about
fifteen feet from the stern. Eventually they cut the line and the gull
tried to fly with the trace and the lead, but he kept losing height
and dropping back into the water. The weight of the lead was too
much for him. In the end I couldn't watch. I went away and when

I came back the bird was gone and the boat was gone. There was only the wind and brutal sea.

My mother was a storyteller. She told us tales of the undersea, of people who had fallen in love with the big dark eyes of the seal and the smooth body, people who forgot that their element was air. They were lost to their families and friends, and even when, occasionally, someone found a sea woman in a net and brought her home, the undersea was always drawing her back, especially at the spring tides when the sea was full and round as a belly. She told us these things at night, when everything is more important, and outside the sea snored among the caves and arches and the curlews called. She told the stories from one or other of our beds, with the blankets pulled up to her chin because her toes were always cold, taking each bed in turn. We three children always fought over whose bed was next. She would turn out the light, and sometimes there was moonlight and sometimes there was none. She began every story in the same way: My mother told me. So that we came to believe that only women knew these things. And perhaps we were right. And in addition, we thought that a story so ancient had to be true, at least in ancient times, however changed the world was in ours. I remember the moonlight slanting in across the room, her low soft voice, Em's breathing. Sometimes Flanagan the cat was there, curled up on the end of the bed.

But one summer there was a fisherman and he would come and drink whiskey after he had set his pots. He was a tall, handsome man. His face was dried and grained by the sea. His eyes had the wind in them, such a blue as you see on dry hard days. My mother welcomed the company and I think he wanted her, or wanted her presence. He never came when Richard's yawl was anchored in the bay. He had been ten years in the boats, he said, in the fleets on the North Sea. The cod fisheries were dying. The Grand Banks were empty. He told us of times when he had been sent aloft to chip ice from the mast lest they capsize with the weight of it. More than once I saw him catch my mother's hand. And she let him do it. She was like that. She was a generous person and touch was a kind of generosity to her. But he came only that one summer. Maybe he died. Or maybe he could not bear to be near her and not have her. Or maybe he went back to sea. He too told stories. He told us that the sound between us and The Calf was haunted. They had all seen a ship there once, in a place where no ship could go because of the shoal. His grandfather had been fishing there another night long ago and whatever he saw or heard he would never say, except that something put a stone in his belly and he failed away, and his skeleton came through his body before he died.

Em was terrified and fascinated by his stories. Once she said to me that she had seen the bones of the fisherman's grandfather. She said Jeannie had brought them wrapped in her sweater and Richard had put the man together on the kitchen table. She still had one of the bones, she said, in a secret place. She wouldn't tell me where it was but I found it easily enough in a hollow in the trunk of an apple tree. There was a brass ring there, too, and a metal toy soldier. I left them where I found them. I wonder if they're still there or if the tree has healed over. Trees do that. Someday someone will cut it down and find the bone, the ring, and the tin man.

My mother never prayed, she was the least religious person I have ever met, she had not a fingernail of superstition in her, but on the nights of the worst storms she thought the ghosts of the island and the gods of the ruined hearths of the empty houses had turned on her for her betrayals and they would rear the sea up against her and drown her children and herself. We thought it natural for someone to be so fearful. The storms terrified us, too. But she was a grown woman. She should have known better.

Whom did she betray? In her grubby flat on the Kingsland Road, in the days when she was quietly planning her escape, she pointed and said, You most of all. Meaning me. And then she named my sisters Jeannie and Em, Richard Wood, herself. She did not mention my father.

She traveled backwards and forwards to the land in our boat. When we heard the distinctive sound of the Seagull engine, the boat coming round Cuas Point and breasting the seas, we would run down to the pier. We wondered what she might bring.

She was an eavesdropper and loved repeating things overheard in the town or on the bus. She had a wry sense of humor. She had her favorite sayings: she got a lovely death, is it yourself is in it, she's out with me over it, he's great with her this past two years, I'm not myself at all, he gave me the going-on strips. They reappeared later in Richard's poems and he was praised for his natural ear. We used to carry the things she bought—fresh vegetables, socks, batteries—as if they were some precious treasure, as indeed all things are on an island. But her to-ing and fro-ing had a darker side too. I recognize it now in retrospect. At the time it did not seem so.

On one trip ashore she found an article in the *Irish Times* that said science was predicting a new Ice Age. She read it to us that evening. She seemed to think the ice was coming soon. She made a list of warm things we had in the house, woollen vests and sweaters, blankets and coats and bobble hats and mittens and gloves. Then she made a list of things we would need to buy. She was writing at the table and the electricity was out again, but there was enough light in the western sky. She made her list and she wrote it out fair and said we would go to town the next day and draw down whatever my father had put in her bank account and buy the necessaries. Cold would not catch us sleeping, she said, we would be ready. I can see her clearly, writing frantically, rushing around to check that things were where they were supposed to be, talking all the time. Then, for no good reason, she gathered the three of us and sang us a song her mother used to sing. There were three sisters went to school, all around the loney-o, they spied a lady at a pool, down by the greenwood side-o. It was a cruel song and it always frightened us, but we thought of the whole thing as normality, as the way families were, because we had no experience of any other. When the song ended she told me solemnly that when I was inside her she wondered what she would do. She did not want me, she said, but the minute I was born she could hardly imagine how she would do without me. Then she made us all promise that if the Ice Age came again we would struggle together as a family. She believed that children should be told everything, that they should be treated as adults, that we needed as much information as possible to survive. Next morning there was no more talk of going shopping against the cold. It was a close damp morning and the spiders' nests in the furze were glassy with the night's rain.

She was rolling out bread as I came downstairs, watched warily by Flanagan the cat, and she was still humming the song. When she saw me she nipped a piece of dough and held it to me on her finger. It's for you, Grace, she said, because you're mine.

She sang:

There is a river wide and deep,
All around the loney-o
'Tis there the babe and mother sleep,
Down by the greenwood side-o.

We three sisters had separate lives. Jeannie liked to build elaborate cities in the sand. She dammed inlets with stones and tried to hold the sea back, anxiously anticipating the rising tide, rushing here and there to stop a hole. Once at low water springs she built a wall across a narrow inlet and packed it with sand. I think the moment she loved best was the breach, the water tumbling in, the crumbling sand and shifting stones. She used to watch it in a kind of anxious ecstasy. I thought she would grow up to build things.

In reality Em was the wildest of us all. I see her now chasing the cat around the house, trying to catch his tail. The cat eventually escapes through an open window. Outside it is late afternoon or early evening. There are seals on the rocks. I can hear their barking. My mother never intended to have her, as she often told us. In fact, only Jeannie did not come under that anathema. Em was my accident, she used to say. But neither of us knew how a child could be accidental. Em could walk among the sheep without disturbing them as if she were already a ghost. The cat followed her like a disciple. She brought home an injured blackbird. Look after Em, my mother used to say, and we had to take it in turns, but we were careless and Em was good at hiding. She learned to swim on her own and never told anybody. She might have learned to fly like the shearwaters skimming the waves, but time was against her. She was small enough and her bones were as light as the hollow bones of a bird. I think she was fearless and careless and heedless of everything. I think nothing surprised her. She talked so rarely we never really knew. But sometimes at night she crawled into my bed and slept with her nose between my shoulder blades. In the morning there would be a damp patch in my nightdress. And she slept with her fists bunched as though one day she might need to fight.

I was the curious one. Once I found my father's old store of rabbit snares. Although snaring is mentioned in his first book as a time-honored way of getting food, the outcry from what he called the Cruelty to Everything Except Humans Brigade made him remove it from subsequent editions. Anyway, he had never mastered the technique. Truthfully, he was a poor hunter but he was a good gatherer. The snares were little hoops of steel with a

seized eye spliced into the strands at one end and a steel peg for
anchoring the trap at the other. He may have made them himself.
Or the seizing might have been Richard's work, he did his own
splicing. All that summer I hunted. I set them at places where the
runs went between stones or bushes. I experimented with height.
After a time I stopped handling them with my bare hands because
I would leave my smell on them. I found a pair of white nylon
gloves in my mother's drawer. I decided she didn't need them. I
sat on the highest point of the island in the evening when the rabbits came out to play. The frantic movements of a trapped rabbit.
The bucking and tearing and slow dying. I skinned them myself,
though for a long time I was just hacking and tearing. I only ever
managed to cure a single hide. Lying gutted on a plate they looked
like dead babies. Their flesh purple under the translucent bitter
membrane. Their small mouths. But now I think there was something sexual in the killing and the stripping and in the bare flesh
with its hind legs spread.

Once I was out on the heather looking at my traps and I saw
Jeannie watching me. She didn't know I saw her. She followed me
to each trap and watched me kill two rabbits. I got angry when
I saw her the second time. I chased her and knocked her down.

What are you snooping for?

I wasn't snooping. I wanted to see how you did it.

I looked at her. She was excited. We had been running, of
course. Perhaps it was that.

Em never ate them. She frustrated my hunting by finding my
traps and stamping on them. Once I caught her trying to free
a trapped rabbit. But even she couldn't find everything. And I
forgave her.

How long did we live there? How did we get there? In some families there are archivists to record the significant events, but in ours

there were none. My mother remembered only what she wanted to remember and what she could not forget and my father committed his memories to paper and never wanted to hear about them again. He wrote them in such a way that they became inventions, remote from our experience. We could not recognize ourselves in them, or more accurately, we tried, and failed, to shape ourselves into them. And in time he stopped writing about us because we could no longer be recycled. This is the inevitable consequence of writing things down.

Certainly, by the time I was old enough to remember things we were already there. I remember that they had a gate across the doorway through which I could see the world. When my sisters came along and I was old enough to come and go I saw that this gate was, in fact, a painted fireguard. Where were my sisters born? It is clear that we did not live on the island all the time. There were times when we lived in the city. My mother told me once that my sisters were both born in the old Mothers' Hospital in London. I was born there too, she said. It may or may not have been true—she was not entirely reliable at the time. And I never could reconcile it with what I knew of her life. It must have meant she lived in London for ten years or so.

It's gone now. Years later, when we lived together in her Kingsland flat, we went out to see the building. It looked like a private house. It had the words *The Mothers' Hospital (Salvation Army)* on the front. Why were we born in a Salvation Army hospital? Because that was the way we lived, she said. And that was all she would say. She liked her secrets. The letters, it seems now, were as big as windows. Why did she want to see it? She told me that her three pregnancies were the happiest days of her life. My father was attentive to her, solicitous, and faithful. He was never with anyone else when she was pregnant, and as long as she was breastfeeding he stayed with her. People were so kind. Richard brought her flowers and fruit. When I was born he took her photograph sitting in a pale pink bed jacket, holding me in her arms. There were apples and roses. He still had that photograph, she said, but she had lost her copy. She was always losing things. She said that we should have been happy children, because her happiness was in her milk. We should have been happy, secure, loving people but we were not. She said she could recall each of our faces exactly as we looked up at her from the breast. Each one was different and beautiful and ancient.

We took the bus out and we went past the stop and got out in Hackney and waited for the next bus back so I saw the place of my birth coming and going and on each occasion all I could think of was my mother's happiness and fulfillment, how having a child at her breast made her feel useful. It was a hurtful discovery. I was angry because in a way she was betraying what had happened in the meantime, our grief and our silence. But I kept my anger to myself. It would have served no purpose.

We certainly lived on the island through several springs and summers, and parts, at least, of two winters. We had a boat, an old salmon yawl that took water at a steady pace, steadily sinking all its life. When we got into it there was always water under the boards and sometimes above them. We bailed with Heinz bean cans. The engine was a British Seagull Century longshaft that never failed. It smoked and sounded like a machine gun. Mother went out to the mainland; we rarely went. She went once a week when she could. Sometimes a boatman came out with things we ordered from the shops. When the weather was bad we stayed at home and lived on short rations. Sometimes our money ran out. Or she gave it away. Occasionally we all went ashore. My mother planned these outings. I remember a tinker woman begging on the street. My mother gave her a ten-shilling note—an enormous amount of money. I'm sorry, I have no change. God bless you, lady, it's too much.

Or sometimes we made a run for it and moved ashore for the duration. Crouched in our anoraks, our woolly hats, our Wellington boots, our backs turned to the incoming spray and green water, we laughed and thought we were having an adventure. Then we stayed with Richard Wood and watched the rain sweep across the distant rock that was our home. How old was Richard Wood then? He can't have been more than thirty-five, but he seemed to us to be old, as old as the house and its privileges, its ancient arrogant windows. Tiraneering was his house. It means "the land of iron" in Irish. The cat came with us everywhere we went and Richard hated him. I hear him say: I found him asleep in the laundry, He pissed in the kitchen for Jesus' sake, That fucking cat ate our supper, You pay more attention to the cat than me. And once he had lambs' kidneys in a bowl on the table and they disappeared—the cat farted urine smells all night. Em laughed at that. Flanagan stinks, she said. But Richard put him outside.

Sometimes Father brought us with him to London. He had that Kingsland flat where my mother would eventually die. In those days it was practically in Essex, the farthest, bleakest reach of northeast London. There was a pub on the ground floor. The railway station was a hundred yards away. There was a kebab house across the street. It was like the center of the world and we were weary explorers just come from the periphery where we had witnessed marvels too elaborate to tell. We were the sorry end of that peculiar 1960s invention, the jet-set. We were feckless and lived in several places at once, as they did, but our mode of transport was a salmon yawl, a ferry, a train. We were their inverse image.

At any rate, he was famous by then, having appeared on television as the bestselling author.

We heard him more than once on the World Service when we could get it, which depended on the disposition of the atmosphere above our heads, whether we could catch what Richard Wood called the sky-wave or not. We imagined him coursing in on a long swell between the grey and the blue skies, above the clouds. We heard our names.

We thought of him traveling in something very like Richard Wood's *Iliad*. Mother said he was a traveling preacher. She said if ever the world was going to change it would not be because we grew our own vegetables. It would be because people walked away from the bosses. I didn't know who the bosses were.

His stories seemed just like stories to us, like fairy tales. The reality was a few lines of salt-blanched kale. The reality was trying to rot seaweed for fertilizer and having to live with the sour fish smell. Agriculture practiced at the most desultory level. We had no animals except the cat. The reality was being mostly cold at night and then being too hot. And being alone and not knowing how to behave when we were not alone. Of feeling safe with the world's ocean as our moat, a place where no one watched us with envy. A place that was precarious and fatal and temporary. The reality was a kind of foolishness that was like a dream, an existence that had no outside, no edge, that we could never transgress. A dream is a language; it has its own alphabet. But the dream knows that someone somewhere will understand and all communication is founded on that premise. But we grew up without that faith. We never knew that we could be understood. These are the consequences of living on an island.

That last summer I think we sailed almost every day. It must have been an exceptional year. At any rate that's how I remember it. The cockpit of Richard's boat was too small for five of us—Richard Wood, Mother, my sisters, and me. It was narrow and our feet crossed in the center and the huge iron tiller extended two feet, so that whoever sat opposite the helmsman might as well have been steering too.

There was one day that I always think of as the beginning of the end. It was time winding up. Of course I believe that the past is not a narrative, it has no beginning and end, even though we survive, we hold ourselves together by telling stories about ourselves. For a practicing psychologist I have a weak faith in consequence.

We beat out against a southerly wind and we fished for mackerel all day. We caught only three. The shoals were not in so it must have been June or early July. We hove to about ten miles out and we three children lined the rails and dropped our lines and Mother and Richard Wood held their faces to the sun and chatted. When they had had enough, he backed the staysail and brought her round and we sailed back, surfing thunderously on the ingoing swells. The boat rushed forward, caught in the belly of one, and then, unable to keep pace, slowed and fell back into the next following trough. In the valleys the sails flogged and clapped, and on the crest they were full-breasted matrons shooing us home. Mother and Richard Wood took turns at the tiller. They sat very close. I saw that he held her right thigh tightly between his knees. His body was moving with the movement of the boat. Her knee was in his groin.

Her knee in his groin and the motion of the boat and the scissors of his thighs around hers. It was a slow warm day and I was thirteen and at that point it was an easy thing to fall. In those days I swam so much my skin ached. I tasted salt. I was holding the mizzen shroud in one hand and my mackerel feathers in the other. It was simply a matter of transferring my trust from the boat to the line. I fell over the stern. I surfaced quickly. I could feel the tug of the lead. Had a mackerel caught the feather he could have towed me away and I would not have cared. I saw the boat disappear in a trough and when it rose again they were looking for me.

Swimming in the deep sea is a kind of letting go. I could do it because I was never afraid of anything. The darkness was between my legs. I lost a sandal. The boat came back. It was an elegant piece of seamanship. I know he never for a moment believed I had fallen. But I had.

They made me take my clothes off and sit on the bunk in a towel. My mother put the kettle on. Tea would warm me, she said, as she always did. I had given her a fright, but I was a brave girl. She was an innocent, in so many ways; she trusted things to be themselves. My sister Jeannie came down to look at me. She said nothing. My sister Em looked in and asked if I was all right. She too had been worried. Richard watched me from the tiller. I saw that I had moved the stone of his attention. Sunlight slanted in from the porthole. After a time the primus needed to be pumped again. I did it. When the kettle boiled my mother made tea. There was barely enough room in the tiny cabin for the three of us. She was stooped because the headroom was bad.

They hung my clothes on the guardwire and as we approached the anchorage they gave them back. They were damp and sticky.

Richard said I would need to learn that there was always one hand for the boat and one for myself. He said I was such an otter that I needed to learn how to stay out of the water. I needed to become truly amphibian. I suspected he was preparing a poem in his head and these random metaphors were some kind of a beginning.

Em let the anchor go. She liked lifting the pawl and releasing the clutch with the iron bar. It was something a child could do and love. Lift the pawl and release the clutch and the chain runs out with a satisfying clatter that becomes a growl. Tighten the clutch again. She loved it. The wind was almost gone. We came to a slow stop, winding the jib on the Wykeham-Martin gear. The mizzen was always first to go up, last to come down. It kept her nose to the wind, he said. The bay was ablaze in the evening sun. There was a seal watching us. He put me and Jeannie ashore first and then went back for the others. We walked up to the house.

Jeannie said, I saw you, you jumped.

I did not.

I saw you letting go.

I changed in our room up under the slates and when I came down they were all there in the kitchen. Richard had the mackerel. He ran his knife along the membrane of the belly and the guts spilled out red and black. He nipped the stomach where it penetrated the gut and scraped it into a bucket and started again. My mother had her hands in the basin. She brushed soil from the potatoes with her thumbs. They were laughing. They were talking in low voices but still I heard what they were saying. They were talking about running away. Outside it was already dark. Jeannie was at the window looking out at the reflection of the inside, as though she could see through it. Em was looking into a picture book. Nobody looked at me.

I see now that I was already watching my mother for the secrets she knew, even though in the end it would be Jeannie who mastered them; they were wasted on me. I knew it was her body. I remember her beautiful breasts with their sand-pale aureoles, the wrinkle under them, her full straight thighs and the place between them. Though I didn't know it then, I wanted my body to know such things.

The longer my father stayed away the more open she became with Richard. She kissed him holding her palm flat against his heart. What did her hand hear? I watched them lying in a fold of heather near the beacon facing the sun. She was listening. What was he saying? I would never know. Her summer frock was turned back to her hip. She liked the heat but she never tanned. Her face was freckled but pale. The beacon threw a long shadow. When it reached them they got up.

I listened for their lovemaking all that summer long. But what can be learned from listening tells us nothing about gesture or act. Although what happens is natural enough, no one could invent it, exactly. I knew all about whispering and sighing and hushing and the other sounds. Their bed creaked like a boat.

On my birthday, he gave me a poem. Jeannie gave me a stone shaped like a seal with one eye. Em gave me a card with our names in a heart.

We were sitting at the table. I looked at the poem as if I were reading but in reality I was watching my chance. When Mother turned to the kitchen I kissed him on the mouth. It tasted of fat. Mother never saw but Jeannie did. Her jet-black eyes. What was the poem about? I tore it up that night. I never read a word. That night I hated him for sitting there and accepting my kiss and saying nothing to break her spell. When she turned around she was holding my birthday cake on a plate. There were only two candles—I don't think we ever had any more—and he began that idiotic fellow song and they all joined in the chorus. I should have known that he was a failure but children only feel the horror. They have no idea why.

When we had eaten the cake we all went out to see the evening. I remember that the sun was a blood orange and there were thin lines of horizontal cloud. I remember it more intensely because of my state of mind. If it had been raining I would remember it as clearly because everything I saw and felt that evening had the intensity of sex. We walked to the western end of the island and my mother, with Richard's help, climbed onto the beacon. She was triumphant and a little crazed. Up there, she said, she would have sunshine long after we were in darkness. Em cried because she was

jealous. Em was the climber in the family. I walked down to the
pebble beach with Richard. He said, You must take care of your
mother, Grace. He was thoughtful, and I think, a little frightened. I
knew what he meant. He turned to look back when he said it, and
I looked too. She looked like some kind of stone against the dark-
ening sky, a graven image as unsafe and uncertain as any false god.

And then there was a scene in our kitchen some days or weeks
later. My mother stood with her back to the sink and her arms
folded. She wore, I remember, a long patterned caftan. The pat-
tern was a kind of red paisley like an amoeba on a pale cream.
She wore slacks and sandals. Her face was freckled. Her hair was
held back by a band of tortoiseshell. She was never more beautiful than when she was angry. Em was somewhere else. She may
have been upstairs. Jeannie was sitting by the window. She had
been to the well, I remember, and the bucket of water she had
brought was standing on the kitchen floor. I could see a fine membrane of dust and pollen and salt gathering on it in the sunlight.
Richard Wood stood in the center of the room talking about me.
I needed some discipline in my life, he said. I was growing up.
Sooner or later I would leave the island and I would have to make
my way in the world. I remember he said it exactly like that, in
those old-fashioned terms: I would have to make my own way in
the world.

It was as though I weren't there, but I was. Or at least I think
I was. It's true that Jeannie remembered it for me. She told me
everything in careful detail many years later, including things I
didn't know about. She was able to tell me that Richard talked
about their plan. He was to take me out sailing and explain everything. He was to do it gently, in a fatherly way, there being no
father to speak of at that moment. Out there, alone with me, on
the waste of the sea.

Jeannie remembered that he had blue jeans with a slight flare and that he had a faded blue fisherman's smock. He could wear those things authentically. It was as though his class had appropriated the entire history of the country and could be what they liked, whatever character from fiction or history: the poor beggar, the journeyman tailor, the wandering seaman, the sailor. We saw them wherever we went, in London, in the houses we visited, these members of the former ruling class who had adopted victimhood as though it belonged to them.

In the end my mother agreed. She agreed, I think, because she could not do without him. If my father had been there it would never have happened. But there were long weeks when we were alone. When we saw Richard's sails—and they were unmistakable: two headsails, one set on a bowsprit with the ancient Wykeham-Martin winding gear, the tall main, the little stunted mizzen, the classic yawl-rig; there was no other boat like it on the coast at that time— our hearts lifted. Here was news of the main. Here was someone with stories to tell, with fruit or meat or newspapers or Kiley's lemonade.

All right, she said. I give in. But you must be back by teatime. No wandering.

She meant he could not keep me away after dark. She knew he sometimes drifted up the coast and stayed offshore during the night. That he fished and drank black coffee. That he sometimes found himself among the night trawler fleets, or out where the big companies were prospecting for oil. Or anchored in some cove out of the seaway. She would not stand for that. Not the two of us alone in the boat overnight, the sea and the stars and the two of us in the little cabin in the afterheat of the primus stove.

I don't think she believed in any plan. Childhood was nothing to her. It was just another time.

So I picked up my anorak, my boots, my jumper and went down with him to the boat.

We would sail south for half the day. At midday we would turn and beat back up. At that point we would be twenty-five or thirty miles offshore. It would be him and me and the deep sea. A sailboat is all protocol and procedure, he said. And the names of things. He named each rope, each stay and shroud, each of the corners of the sails, each edge, each block and its tackle and parts, the sheave, the cheek, the choke, the cleat. He named the processes of taking in and letting go. In the brutal simplicity of that day he named things I have never forgotten. I remember that unless the mizzen was trimmed properly she sailed like a bitch. I remember that he had stitched a leather cutaway into the clew of the inner staysail and the threads had worked loose. I remember that in light airs it was necessary to back the jib to make her tack and that unless it was done smartly the boat simply stopped in irons. All this I learned, and so much more.

The leaving and the return are the boat's best time. She feels the anchor coming home and she becomes impatient for the sea. She is at her slowest and most sensitive. She turns her head. The wind against her body.

First the mizzen. He showed me how to sweat it up. Even for someone with my light frame it was easy work. We unwound the jib and when the anchor was home and dry he allowed her to fall away to one side and used the backed headsail to turn her to the open sea. Once outside the arms of the anchorage he brought her to wind and I sweated the main and the staysail and we bore away. He told me what to do and I must do it at once. There was never to be time to think. I must carry out each order quickly, precisely, calmly. Mistakes would be punished by the boat.

This is what we did.

It was a brilliant day of northerly winds. The sea in the lee of the land was flat. The sails filled and the boat ran out, and all that long day he drove me to distraction.

Far out beyond the horizon there were only two of us. The wood giving to the wind and sea. Wooden boats move in every way.

He told me my mother was worried about me.

His arms around the iron tiller. There was a knuckle of iron at the end. One hand enclosed it.

Did I know that they had talked about sending me to board at his old school? It was co-ed now. My father had been written to. I was a wild child. My mother had asked him to take my reading in hand and so I might be seeing more of him. He said that my father's theories about homeschooling were fine when I was younger, but now I would need to sit exams. I would need to think about the future. It was a cruel world, he said, and wildness was punished without mercy. He had been thinking a lot about me, he said, and so had my mother. Worrying, in fact. They had both been worrying about me.

I had not known I was in danger. I sat straight as a larch, staring at the future that seemed to me no more than several wave crests distant. I would leave the island. She wanted to part us. I hated her for it. She was plotting to put me aside. When children think of punishing their parents they understand what it is to be powerless. They think about dying. *When I'm dead you'll be sorry.* I tried to imagine such a complete punishment. But I also knew I would not be there to know. Then later there was fear. What would school be? What were other people of my age like?

All this as we ran down our southing with nothing but the heaving sea before and the land falling away behind. He watched me. In the dreamy running down when the boat ran almost as fast as the wind and it seemed as if we were carrying our own air, the sails full of it, wing on wing.

I was long and straight from shoulder to hips. My shorts hung low. At some point in my anger and fear I became conscious of the dimpled hollows of his back and waist.

His arms wrapped around the iron tiller, his cheek on his shoulder. He had long lashes like a girl's. The sinews of his arms. His hair fell continually into his eyes and he brushed it away with a gesture that took five hundred years to perfect.

And coming back he shouted and hectored me. Each tack was a welter of rope and clattering sail and groaning blocks. We beat up hard by and water flew in our faces. He worked me brutally, coldly. My muscles hurt. My skin burned from the sheets. Now I know what he was doing. He was loosening my grip on myself.

By evening we were anchored in the Carthys, two broken reefs with a patch of drowned sand between. We were stopping there to eat, he said. In an hour or so the wind would shift and set fair for home. We would coast back on the evening breeze. My mouth was dry. My nails were broken. I was mortally tired. I said I would bathe before eating. I began to change into my swimsuit. I moved swiftly, peeling things away, dropping them. My shirt, my shorts, my pants.

Use a towel, he said. But it was too late.

Look at you, he said, you're brazen.

He smelled of sweat and iron. I was pulling on my bathing suit, I think. I stopped and looked him straight in the eye. What if he kissed me? My head to his? I kept my mouth closed. He would put his hand on me. Now something in my belly leaped like a fish. My heart raced. He looked at my face. I stared brazenly at him, covered barely to the waist, the straps of my bathing suit trapped between finger and thumb of each hand. I saw him look down. I knew what he was looking for. I remembered my mother's muffled cry in the night, the sound of animals struggling. There was an instant that hung at the cusp, when anything might have happened, I believe that still.

Then he slapped me.

I was taut and supple as a whiplash. I went straight out onto the little afterdeck. I thought for an instant of jumping. I believed in swimming away, in striking out for home, five or six miles of open sea. I could trust myself to the ocean. I stretched my arms towards it, arched my back, my toes wrapped on the coaming. Already I was exulting in falling. It would have fixed the moment forever. But he called out.

Don't, he said. Stop as you are.

I turned to defy him. For the first time ever I was conscious of my breasts. They were small—they still are—but the nipples were pale, something like the color of sunlit sand. It occurred to me that there was power in staying as well as running away.

I'm going to jump, I said.

You'll only have to come back. There's nothing on these rocks.

Someone would come. Mum would come.

Who would tell her?

I could swim.

I'll write a poem about you, he said.

He could do the little-boy look. He had that grace and simplicity. And he could be sad.

It might have turned my mother's head, but not mine. I shrugged. I didn't like poems. He had left several in our house for safekeeping at various times. They were memorials of his days here, vignettes of our lives, love poems to a family that was not his. I didn't think they were important. We always lost them.

He said, You could be a boy or a girl.

I didn't know how to understand that. Was it good or bad? What I felt was shame.

I shook my head.

Come and put your clothes on. Let's go home.

Put your clothes on, he said again.

I sulked. But I didn't jump. He nodded once, as though he had read my thoughts. I watched him go below.

My eyes were heavy. Everything went in phases, slow as water. He pumped the primus. The sharp smell of the paraffin. The pop of the flame. My legs felt too long, like an animal's. An eland or a gazelle. And we sat at opposite ends of the cockpit. We had bread and cheese and tea. I folded one knee onto the other as my mother did, slanted my legs away. It was a warm, still evening. The breeze that would take us home was slow in coming. He watched me from under his lashes. I felt free and dangerous, as though I had hurt him. When the night breeze finally blew I left that reef full of pleasure and power. I remember standing on the bow of the *Iliad* with my legs spread, braced to the inner forestay, the wire pressed into my skin. Afterwards my arm and side were flecked with tar where the strands left their mark. The breeze was in my face then. If he had asked me I would have given him everything. It might have been a world, a universe, a way of life—I didn't know what would be required of me, but I knew it was vast. There were no discernible tracks. The mountain sheep knew the way, those that came to the island. The seabirds on the cliffs knew. The seals, the dolphins, the fin whales. Their sinuous bodies found the seaway without pain. Now I wanted to know more than anything what his body would feel like. What would come next? Where would he go?

Later Jeannie told me that they had talked about me and that my mother said I was becoming a woman. I said I thought that's what I had always been, that it just meant I wasn't a man. But Jeannie instinctively knew that it was something else, something more important and that there was something dangerous in it, that I should be afraid. When I didn't react she told me it was raining outside and did I want to play draughts? She listed the other games we could play. Ludo, snakes and ladders, dominoes, Junior

Scrabble—which Mother was keen on but we were not. I ignored her. I was pretending to be reading, but I knew that Jeannie was right. This would be my last year of freedom. I knew all about schools. I had read *The Highland Twins at the Chalet School* and *Hard Times*. There was something cold and hard in the pit of my stomach that must have been dread. Facts, facts, facts—that was the future to which I would never belong.

She jumped on the bed beside me. She knew what she was doing. She was always the bringer of bad news. She leaned over my shoulder so that her face was against mine. Her skin was dry and hot. Her breath smelled yeasty.

They're sending you away, she said. They're going to send you to school.

My father never came all that remained of the summer and my mother, as I remember it, never once spoke about him. Nor did she mention school. I came to believe that if I was a good girl nothing more would happen. I could stop the arrow in flight.

All this happened to us as I remember it, things we had no right to expect, wonders and minor miracles and also terrible things. We children tried to find our way in this world of edges that proliferated into chaos, and I suppose the adults were navigating too. Only the cat knew everything.

Jeannie

It's Grace's day to look after Em. She and Em are down at the western beach searching for soft-belly crabs under stones to bait hooks with. They have a bucket for them and the bucket is filling with scrabbling green and brown machines. It's a summer's day. I'm wandering on the western end of the island looking for bright stones or bits of quartz. I find the bones of a seabird in a wall. I brush the bones out with a feather, they're so light. They're chalk fine, so fragile I think they might turn to dust in my hands. I brush them onto my sweater, lay them out on the heather below and begin to put them together again. I feel a terrible sense of loss, as if the bird is mine, a pet or one that was nesting under my window. Birds, like humans, seek out shelter in bad times. We all need a niche in a wall to hide ourselves in, to get well again, or to die. I'm so lost in setting the bones back in place that I miss the clouds building out from the mainland, the distant thunder. When the downpour begins I'm taken completely by surprise and for a time in the noise and the battery of the rain I'm completely flummoxed. Eventually I bundle the bones into my sweater and run for home.

Richard is there.

Jane is lying down upstairs.

He laughs. Look at you, we have to get you out of those clothes, you'll catch your death of cold.

He peels them off one by one and wraps me in a towel and I stand there like a stick insect, a gangly, bony, shivering child and he holds me tight and scrubs me. All our towels are ruined by salt. They're coarse and unbending. I think he scoured my skin away and penetrated to my heart. He could have seen it beating steadily, contentedly, if he had bothered to turn me 'round.

When I'm dry he kisses me on the top of my head and slaps my bottom. Get into something dry, he says, go on now, you silly child. Words of endearment. Sometimes he calls me that still. Come here to me, silly child.

When I come out again he's opened my bundle of bones. He's spread the sweater on the kitchen table and Grace is there and they're speculating about the structure and function of the bits and pieces. The bones in their hands. This one fits here. If we put that there then these two go together. Suddenly I hate her. I stand there and watch her taking my place and I have nothing to say. Em comes over to watch too, her thumb in her mouth she studies the bones. The rain outside the window is straight down without wind to slant it, a grey curtain that closes off the entire ocean. The air in the house feels colder and cleaner. I go upstairs and pick up one of Grace's books. I can't remember what it was now, she was always reading. I climb onto a chair and open the roof window and put the book outside on the slates. The sea is furious, explosive, frightening. The small cove is full of water even though it should be only half tide. There's a boiling yellowish scum all along the edges, sticks, seaweed, a glass pot buoy, a milk crate. Rain. The house is drowning in static. The light becomes steel. The blank windows.

Flakes of memory from a nugget of malachite that is the unknowable past. But none of us has a whole memory anyway, whatever we think. What we hear others tell us permeates our understanding. Their thoughts run like subterranean streams in ours. Never trust anyone who has a simple tale to tell.

Jeannie loves stones—I've heard them say that about me since I was a child. It usually feels like a joke, something complicated implying that I find it hard to love people. But of all the family, I'm the lover, the faithful lover of people. Still, it's true stone is my passion. When I was a girl I wondered why in certain places the rocks lay flat, in others sloped and in others curved, why some stones are round and others sharp. These are simple questions but the answer is as complicated as the history of the world. Before ever I came to study geology I'd formed my own theories about how the ground under my feet came to be. Once in a secondhand bookshop I found a topological map and saw that a great wave-train of old red sandstone ran along the coast to the west of our island, with spatters of limestone in the troughs; I saw that the tops of this wave-train were the headlands that I could see marching westward into the sunset, and that the troughs were the bays that the sea had hollowed out of the soft limestone. It was years before I confirmed this impression in a textbook and when I did I was disappointed to find that the theory was not my own, but also quietly pleased at having discovered it for myself.

I was always fascinated by the tides. Where did they start? Why did the moon change them? Richard knew. He drew diagrams at the kitchen table, circles and sine waves and arrows. The great tide wave of the Atlantic runs from the North Cape of Norway where the Atlantic and Barents Sea meet, past Fastnet Rock to the south of us, and back again every six hours, billions of tons of water grinding against the continents and islands—a wave a hundred feet high was recorded not far from our island and they say it was not unusual This vast swirl of water washes the stones at our door and sweeps the ocean bed clear. We lived, in those days, in an iron-bound coast with deep safe harbors, a morphology shaped by folding and fracture as well as by erosion and hydraulic action; we lived in the presence of big round mountains that rose in the distance, old worn mountains shaped by rain and wind, among the islands and their outlying reefs, their sands and their pebble beaches and raised beaches and the fragile remains of human habitation.

Tom is leaving the island tomorrow. Tonight there is the preparation. Mainly he travels with only a large rucksack for his clothes, his manuscript, whatever he is working on at the time. He keeps the manuscript in a plastic bag. I remember that it was a faded olive-green Marks and Spencer's bag. He used to say that Marks and Sparks did the best-quality plastic. Of course it's raining. His oilskins hang stiff as corpses behind the door, ready for the crossing. Em hides her top half behind them and every once in a while looks out to see if anyone has noticed. When she looks I make a face at her and she smiles that slow, secret smile. Peek-a-boo.

Recriminations.

Jane says, I can't manage on my own. When will you be back? What am I going to do for money? Easy for you to say. Do you have any idea what it's like?

Daddy, can I come this time, you promised.

My sister Grace looks on. I think I can feel her contempt but that's probably something I've invented over the years. Certainly she hated all of that. Flanagan stares from his perch on the window; his insouciant eyes say, However it falls out I'll be fed.

Please . . .

Suddenly I see weeks that are like years stretch out before me. Islands are, more than anything else, places of deprivation. How old am I? Six, seven?

I want to go, I want to go, you promised.

I have seen children winding up like that, the mantra of wanting and needing and deserving. In a few minutes it will become a wail. He slaps me. I hear it first and feel it later. It can't have been very hard, he never used force.

Jane says nothing. She sits at the table, the mother figure of a demented folk story, her hair tangled, her fingernails outlined in black, her cheesecloth shirt stiff with salt.

Grace sniggers.

Em winds into his arms and begins to cry.

Following her example I cry too.

I'm sick of here, I wail, I want to go.

Why don't you take her, Jane says.

One of these days . . .

There's no time like the present.

Jesus Christ, this is a madhouse.

Please, Daddy . . . ?

He sits Em on a free chair and kisses her on the cheek. He gets up and goes to the door. The door is open because the rain is soft and the night is cloying-warm. The sea is still out there. In the distance we can hear the foghorn on Fastnet Rock.

He turns suddenly and there is his warmest smile. It radiates everything I ever wanted—love, happiness, comfort, hope. Oh, he was a charmer, he charmed thousands in every corner of the world. I was a child—how could I resist? Come here to me, child, he says. He holds his arms out and I run for them. He wraps them around me.

What will I bring you from America, he says. Will I bring you a red Indian?

Laughing and smothered, held tightly in the oily, sheepy smell of his Aran sweater, I hear Grace's step on the stairs and the door of our room closing.

Oh, you can win them over when you want to, Jane says, easily done when you're only here a few weeks in the season. You don't have to scratch a summer out of this fucking rock. I can't cope any longer. Put that in your next bloody book. It doesn't work, Tom. I'm not going to live the way you want.

I turn in the wheel of his embrace and look at her. I want her to come into the circle too. She is tapping the table with her middle finger, sharp, short raps like a blackbird breaking a mussel shell on a rock. Suddenly she sweeps her hand away and a plate and a cup fly. They break against the wall. She looks at them for a moment, then she begins to rap again.

The watchtower is another somber flake of green in my box of memories.

I go there to play a game I call chainies. This game never includes Grace because Grace is outside everything. I don't know where I learned the game. It was as if games grew naturally from the landscape and their names were inherently exact. I have bits of old china, broken plates and saucers, cups without handles, but also certain beautiful stones and pieces of seaworn glass. I have fragments of those old glass buoys they used to mark lobster pots, the most beautiful green blasted to jade by the action of the sea. Sometimes my chainies are things in a shop. Sometimes I serve tea in them to my menagerie of toys, a bear with one eye, a donkey without a tail, a small monkey. I've trodden down something like a hare's sett inside the ruined walls of the watchtower, the weeds all laid out in the counterclockwise direction I first walked them. There's no wind in there. Sometimes I hear a gale grumbling over the walls, the sea grinding against the cliff. I see seabirds blown away on the wind's wings. But inside is my own private calm, a constant storm's eye, my own world.

I hear a noise. I turn and look to the entrance but there's no one there. Then I see her shadow. Em's shadow. She is perched high on the wall looking down at me. How did she get there? The memory is unsettling. It has no clear beginning or end. Was she there before I arrived? Have I forgotten or repressed some decision to allow her to climb on the forbidden wall? I can't be certain anymore. It has the logic of a nightmare. In memory I am paralyzed by her presence. She sits beside the window with its musket loop, kicking her heels against the stone. Don't go any farther, Em. The window is a whirlpool of emptiness: none of us has passed it. Our heads whirl at the thought.

She doesn't acknowledge that I see her. She is watching the game. She has her thumb in her mouth. Her eyes are big. A child's game is a closely defined world. To step outside for an instant is to see the world vaporize like a dying star.

You're meant to be with Grace, I say, it's her day.

She says nothing, but she inches down on her bottom and runs away.

But Grace plays games too. She invents one that only she can win. First she promises something: to tell something, because she always knew secrets; to give something; to do something. I always want what she has to offer. Then she explains something difficult or unpleasant that I must do to get it. The pleasure she takes in watching my agonized desire, my bargaining, my reluctant acceptance. Grace's game is what passes for fate in my childhood. She knows where a robin is nesting. There are three eggs. If I want to see it I have to tell Jane a lie. I spend days trying to invent a lie that I would be able to tell. Then she brings me to see the nest. She always keeps her promise, that's part of the game. Strands of my black hair and Grace's fair are wound together with grass and leaves and, in the middle, three perfect eggs the color of sandstone. If you mind Em I'll show you the hole where the conger comes out.

That summer there is a great bloom of jellyfish all along the
south and west coasts. They wash in on the sand and we bury them
above the tide line. They are our aliens, palmfuls of colored glass
and string. Grace swims and occasionally emerges with little weals
of sting. She will tell me a secret, I forget what now, if I come too.
From a distance she looks like she's floating on a vast sheet of colored glass. I am too frightened. At night they give me bad dreams.
They come and go on the tide, the earth's phlegmy breathing. Then
one day they're gone forever and it is autumn.

Jane is trying to school us. On one of her trips ashore she picks
up a book about the sea. She wants to use the jellyfish to make us
learn. It is an admirable theory of education. Among other things
she tells us that they have two phases, the polyp and the medusa,
and they reproduce by budding; the life cycle is characterized by
pulses that give rise to summer blooms like the one coming ashore
on our strand. But information comes to us as a kind of pleasant
static from another country, inexplicable, a cipher for which we
have no key but which is beautiful to contemplate. Gradually I lose
my fear. If the bloom returned now I would do it and Grace could
tell me the secret she never revealed. Em has fallen in love with
the words. She has a little song she sings that goes, Polyp, medusa,
bloom, polyp, medusa, bloom. She sings it over and over again. I
hear her singing herself to sleep.

One day a boy comes ashore from a lobsterman's boat. They have
engine trouble. I see them pulling into the western beach, running
the bow onto the shingle. It is a dangerous entrance, a sharp reef
with a narrow gap. Only a local could find his way in. Together
they take the cowling off the outboard and begin taking it apart.
They spread an oilskin coat on the shingle and place the pieces on
it. Flanagan the cat comes down. Whenever a boat lands he sus-
pects fish. He lounges in the sea pinks watching and dozing. After

a time I see that the boy has nothing to do. I go down and ask him if he wants to play. I was a wild child with no idea how to behave with strangers. His father stares at me, but the boy says yes. I'm pleased because he's a big boy and little girls are in awe of big boys.

James Casey is his name. His father is Mike Casey. He is known as Little Jimmy, but I can't call him that. He lives in the village of Rally across the sound.

I bring the boy to the tower and show him my treasures. I explain the game but I can see that he's not concentrating. I scold him for not paying attention. He asks me to show him my knickers. I don't care about knickers but I know the game would never work that way. I refuse and when he tries to catch me I dodge past him easily and up onto the wall. He starts to climb after me. Then he sees the sheer drop on his left-hand side, a hundred feet or more from where we stand to the sea. The water below is clear. He stops climbing.

He tries to get me to come down. I think he's more frightened now than interested in my underwear. From high up over the sea I lift my skirt and show him my knickers and then I stick my tongue out and laugh at him. It is Grace's laugh, the way she can make me feel small. He runs away. I can see him tearing through the thistles and bracken.

I'm excited. For a long time afterwards I tried to think why he wanted me to show and why he thought I would.

We're at Richard's house at Tiraneering. Grace is reading, Em is sleeping in Jane's arms, Richard is closing the big shutters with their brass latches. Tom is there but I do not see him in memory. It's late and we have been playing cards. Who won? It was usually my father. But I cannot remember.

Then we go upstairs, Tom, Grace, Em, Jane, Richard, and I, turning out the lights one by one so that by the time we reach the

top of the stairs there is a huge fissure of darkness at our backs with
Flanagan the cat emerging from it, his eyes of malachite green. He
sleeps with Jane.

These old houses, Richard used to say, they need an empire
to keep them alive. Meaning the portraits of admirals and col-
onels who went out to defend England in the China Sea and
Omdurman. This is Captain Richard Wood, he was with Nelson
at the Nile, he was wounded in the leg by a fragment of iron from
the explosion of *L'Orient*. I loved those stories. Between the col-
onels and admirals, the dead aunts mostly disapproving of what
had befallen them—death and reduced circumstances, retirement,
half pay, the Encumbered Estates Act.

The stupidity of memorial.

Tom standing on the top step with his hands resting on the
balustrade, declaring his objections to all of that: We should have
burned you out like foxes.

Flanagan is cat-sniffing around his feet, his greeting ritual.
Does that mean that Tom has just arrived? Where has he come
from? How long have we been here?

And Richard saying, Nobody burns foxes out, Tom.

My father means the War of Independence, that all the land-
lords should have been driven away. He's against land ownership,
or at least ownership on the vast scale of the Tiraneering estate.
Now they're at it hammer and tongs: the landlord class, the
gombeen class, parasites, reactionaries.

Arguments terrify a child. I've no concept of what a friendly
quarrel might lead to, how friends make fun of each other. To me
it looks and sounds like Grace's game. I have no skin. I'm always
sensitive, in so many ways, whereas Grace has a professional hau-
teur that protects her from the vagaries of love.

Later I can't sleep. I think about fire. I look at the windows to
see how they can be opened. I wonder would I die if I jumped

out onto the stone yard below. There's moonlight, that night or another night, and I see an owl ghosting towards the fields. He seems inflated, enormous. I don't know what he is—I think he might be a soul taking leave of us.

That night or another night there are words about Jane. I don't know what is said—they're always talking riddles. It is Em who wakes us. She says she heard a ghost. She lies in Grace's bed with her eyes wide open, her thumb in her mouth. It's possible only she knew how things would turn out: children and dogs, they say, have that instinct. We listen but hear nothing. Then it comes again, a faint, animal wailing. Then there are doors. First we are happy that the sound is human, then we realize that the silence means we are alone. We close the shutters but it does no good. We hear Flanagan mewling at the door and let him in. We are all terrified but Grace is the worst. Poor Grace. Why is it that without seeing we all know the sequence? They argued, Mother cried, she walked out. It is a dark, cold night. There is no moon and the stars are like broken glass.

We go over the sequence, folding our stories into each other: Grace says there was the wailing and then loud talk and then shouting, I remember the kitchen door banging closed, then there was silence, we are all agreed on that, we all remember the silence. Grace says she heard Jane's voice in the yard so we all go to the window and open the shutters again to look down. We are in time to see Tom and Richard carrying flashlights, going their separate ways, Richard through the gate, Tom by the side of the old stable. They are calling and calling; for a time we can see their lights.

Grace says that if they want to find her they have to leave us alone. If we want our mother back we must wait in the haunted room. Em begins to cry. Mammy is gone, she keeps saying, mammy is gone. Grace holds her in her arms. She'll come back, Em, she says.

Old houses, big houses, make noise, they talk at night in their own fabric language. A million beetles eat. Mice live in the attics and behind the wainscot. Rafters and runners and boards shift in their beds of stone. Lath and plaster wear each other away. Water courses in copper and lead. Every time the house settles itself we hear a pistol shot, a groan. We hear ghosts in the other rooms. Conversations. Noises on the landing.

We fall asleep together—children need sleep more than love and Flanagan is our comforter—Em between Grace and me, none of us knowing what we fear, but fearing that when we wake up everything will have fallen apart, everything will be different. At such times a continuation of even the unhappiest life is preferable to the unknown. We dream, of course, whatever those dreams were, certainly uneasy versions of ourselves. At some point Flanagan gives up and moves out. None of us are awake to hear them bring her back but in the morning she's there to wake us. It's no comfort. She's pale and her eyes are red. For all we know she might be a changeling, a fairy woman. For all we know our mother might have gone into the bog and this is her ghost.

Our island home. What is the house like?

Go through the front door and you're immediately in the kitchen. Flanagan checks your shoes for hostile tomcat smells; he knows there is no other cat on the island. He knows me. You may pass, Jeannie, his insouciance says, you're nothing new. This is the biggest room, with the chimney breast at one end and the stairs to "the loft" at the other. Before we came someone put a black Stanley no. 8 range in the chimney and when it is hot it heats the entire house. Tom told me that when they bought the house there were mice nesting in the open oven. They scampered out when Jane opened the door. She just laughed.

The timbers that hold up the floor above us are solid oak, they look like ship's timbers, and the floorboards above are oak planks too. There is a long tradition of harvesting shipwrecks along this coast. In *Living an Island, Loving the World* Tom told about sea-faring families who buried timber or brass or furniture or brandy and the complicated folk laws that governed found things. It was his most popular book.

Up the narrow stairs, Flanagan at our heels, and there are two bedrooms, each with a "light," a window set into the roof that mainly looked upwards at the sky. Their room has an iron-framed double bed that they kept because Jane said it would be bad luck to throw out. It's heavy cast iron with brass knobs and where it stands there are four hollows in the oak. Flanagan sleeps in the bed, and on bad nights he sleeps underneath among the shoes and cardboard boxes of winter clothes.

Our room has three iron-framed beds, hospital issue, which they picked up when a local hospital was downgraded to an old folks' home. Although the windows are set into the slope of the roof, still by standing close to them I can see down to the shore and across the sound at the sandbar where oystercatchers and turn-stones, curlews and sandpipers live their intertidal days. Wading birds feature strongly around us. Their cries are our nightsongs. Em imitates them. She can do a curlew perfectly. She could call them here from the half-tide flats but what would we do with them?

To furnish the house Jane and Tom and Richard scour the auction rooms. The Irish are throwing out their old mahogany to buy expensive stuff veneered with Formica and there's a ready supply of what people eventually begin to talk of as "antiques." To Tom and Jane they're just the cheapest, strongest, most functional things they can get. One day they buy a deal table for the price of a shirt (Tom's words) and beech chairs, a pine dresser, an oak log box, and a coal scuttle with a cracked tin lining. Another evening they come home in an overladen salmon yawl and disembark with a mahogany armchair, a rosewood lady chair, and a beveled mirror in an art deco frame. In a priest's house, being sold as part of the reforms of the Second Vatican Council, they find a brass-bound barometer and a perfect mahogany sideboard to be shipped out to us in a trawler a week later so that its legs smell of sour fish for weeks. We're picking up the pope's castoffs, Tom says.

They speak of it as furniture but later I recognize it as a political position: they're rejecting capitalism, or at least Jane is, the conventions of rising consumerism, the faith in the new, in favor of the products of unalienated labor. Others might have fetishized the old, the antique. Not Tom and Jane.

It's more of an anachronism now than it was then. In those days there were people like that.

Even as a child I'm fascinated by Richard's body. All the things he did were perfectly elaborated, every action was exact and sufficient. Even the process of swallowing something—a piece of fruit, a sip of whiskey—is beautifully faithful to itself. I long to be as self-contained in everything, to be Miss Jean Wood and not Jeannie Newman, child of the Big House, and not a ragamuffin on an island. When I see him naked for the first time—at seven or eight—I experience none of the shock that children are supposed to feel. Instead I see his leanness, his hair, his sex, his long fingers and loose limbs for what they are, in their proportions, expressions of his personality, the physical poetry of his mind. He's swimming with Jane in the moonlight on a completely calm sea. They're making no sound. It's such a night that even if there were ripples I would hear them. It is, I think, the beach near Tiraneering because there are pebbles underfoot. I don't see them go into the water but I see their heads, the slow gleam of their path, the occasional white arm in the air. When they come back I see he is a god; in the pale moonlight he might be stone. That he should quarrel with Tom over everything was perfectly reasonable then. When they come out, it's Jane who wraps him in a towel. She folds her arms around him as if she were sheltering him. She whispers into his ear. Everyone knows that something whispered directly into your ear is more exciting, more devastating. It is absorbed like oxygen across the blood-brain barrier. There's no defense.

Her hair is long and it hangs wet down her back to her shoulder blades. They turn and I know that they will discover me if I stay where I am. But if I stay I will see more. I can hear Grace's voice in my head. What will they do next? What happens now? Stay and learn the secret and be caught. I run home. By the time they get back I'm in bed practicing the lies I will tell if they notice anything. But they think I'm asleep. Jeannie sleeps like the dead, Jane used to say.

I may be mistaken—it's too late now to know whether the two incidents were really one, the night swim and the first seeing of his body, and I've never dared to ask him. They both belong to the primordial mass of childhood. They are available to me only in this singular form, like erratics carried by glacial time and deposited on this highland. But their meaning for me is crystal clear, reason enough to remember them out of all the blizzard of experience. They mean fear and lust.

Fear and lust.

So I suppose Richard was my first love. His image set in me, stony and recalcitrant as the perfect man, the perfect lover. Some girls fall in love over and over again with variations on their father. Grace would make much of that, it's the psychologist's perfect love affair. But I skipped whatever necessary anguish was required and fell in love with my father's best friend. A misdirected oedipal urge? A transfer of affection from the taboo subject? I find psychology tiresome, a kind of literary criticism of dreams and chance utterances masquerading as science. The chemical formula for calcium carbonate is $CaCO_3$. Show me a single observation in psychology that's as clear as that. There are none. Science has thousands.

Here is something that I remember in exact detail: it's the morning after the night swim—or possibly a different morning. I go into Richard's room and slip into his bed and put my arms around him. I can hear Jane downstairs putting crockery on the table for breakfast. He's asleep on his side. He loosens a little under my grasp. He rolls back into me. The moment of surrender. I'd seen Jane wrapped into Tom like this, Tom opening to her. I'd seen her wheedling him on the strand, tickling his nose with a sea pink, curled into his back with one hand plucking at the hairs of his chest.

I know exactly what I'm doing.

His body warm and musty and full of nightsmells.

Then he senses my smallness and wakes up. How, in his sleep, did an impression of my body form? Did he dream of a child? He wakes and is cross. What are you doing, get out, out of here, go on, what are you doing . . .

I was too young to be able to read the look on his face. Now I wonder what it was. Was he shocked? Frightened? Ashamed? Angry? Hurt? Excited?

He may have thought it was some childish and inappropriate game.

I go back to my own bed.

As I lie shivering in the morning sheets I feel nothing but triumph. I've done something. Something has happened. Children rarely have the feeling that they can cause things. They experience the world as happening to them. I feel as though I've appropriated something of Jane's power. Now I'm a witch too.

He never told anyone.

But later that day—I'm certain of this—he asks me to walk with him. He is going out to meet the farm manager and to see about cattle. It's a September day of showers and sun and we climb gates and cross fields as happy as birds. I remember that I talked a lot. We meet the farm manager and while they walk among the cattle I pick mushrooms. Richard lends me his cap to bring them home. On the way back we disturb a cock pheasant. He rises out of a lane with a clattering like some wild machinery. He flies over our heads, that strange, impossibly heavy and ungainly flight of the pheasant and his amazing barred gold and russet plumage, and disappears into the woods. Richard tells me that the place is called Derrybeg and that in Irish it means "the small wood." He says there is a little sheltered beach nearby called Derrynatra, which means "the wood of the beach," and that the sound between the islands that we can see from where we stand is called Derrynatra Sound. Even then I saw the system of it, and that in one language the place made complete sense and in another it was just noise. I never forgot the relationship between language and landscape. Years later I remember being asked by a colleague how to find a particular geological feature in a place called Mullock. Look for a hill, I said. *Mullach* means a hill.

Richard and I hold hands walking home in the evening sun and I have never been happier before or since. We talk about what we see. It's Eden and there will never be a fall from grace. The world will always be warm in autumn and I will always be a child and he will be kind. That was how I felt that evening. It was Keats's ode—but the Grecian Urn—*Ah, happy, happy boughs! that cannot shed / Your leaves, nor ever bid the Spring adieu.*

But also it's the knowledge that going into his bed has provoked this excess of kindness.

The storm comes with heavy rain. None of us goes outdoors all day. Usually when that happened there were games but Jane and

Tom aren't speaking. Jane is reading in bed. Tom sits at the table under the window, alternately writing and staring at the rain. Em plays with her toys in her concentrated way.

At some point in the morning Jane comes downstairs. She sits beside Em and puts her arm around her.

Did you get your breakfast, Em?

No.

Did you get your breakfast, Grace?

No, Mam, not yet.

She rounds on Tom. His back is to her. She stands looking at him for a while. The gloomy, shabby room full of secondhand things—the clock, the crooked table, the worn shawl that covered the obscene stuffing of the lady chair, the uneven earthen floor, the leaking stove. I realize I'm ashamed of the way we live.

Tom doesn't turn.

You're useless, she says. This is my island, my house. For you it's only an experiment.

Grace looks at me. What does she know? Being a child means never knowing what other people know. I notice that Tom keeps his head down. An ocean is raining down outside, an inversion of the natural order. I would not be surprised to see fish nosing at the glass, or a seal curious about what happens in houses.

Are you going to grace me with a reply, she says. She waits a while.

That's your answer, then?

Tom is silent. What question is it an answer to? What did they say to each other last night after we fell asleep? In the world of adults everything is bigger. There are things that can never be said although children say them all the time: I hate you; I'm going to kill you; I'm going to spit on you.

Fine, she says, I know where I stand.

She walks out into the rain. She doesn't close the door. She never did when she walked out. I see that she's wearing a shirt and a short pants. I call out to her, Mam, your coat! But she doesn't respond. She doesn't care. It's her island, her home. She'll walk where she likes. For the first time I understand that she doesn't need Tom. The wind drives the rain across the floor. The earth will be mud but the house will still stand, the island holding it together. Grace closes it out.

I saw Jane kill a hen by wringing its neck.

There is a terrible moment of stillness when she pins the bird's wings. I see that the bird is paralyzed by fear, unable to comprehend this new turn of the world. The eyes brown and black, black at the center. I'm frightened to be so close. This frantic mechanism, this heart and talon and feather construction. It smells musty and domestic. She clasps the bird to her breast and with her right hand she finds the neck and, holding the skull in the cup of her palm, twisting her hand in advance so that the movement would be completely natural, she stretches it out and she kills it. There is some fluttering afterwards but nothing much else. The ghost of life remains but the thing is gone. My mother did that without a thought.

Grace has that same pitilessness. I see her with a seagull trapped in one of her rabbit snares. First she tries to catch the bird but it flies at her. Then she kills it with a stone. She detaches the snare and throws the dead bird into a field. I never see her mourn a single dead thing.

There are things I can recall with precision, like when a slide comes into focus in the microscope, a simple adjustment bringing to life a universe in the objective lens. Trivial things come most readily. I remember how clear the sea is on calm days. A distorting mirror. I remember the brackish taste of well water after a storm. I remember Em's thumbnail soft and white from sucking while her other fingers have a fine black sickle under each nail. I remember how Richard hauls a fish straight up out of the water on his handline and lands it into a bucket, how he inserts his thumb and forefinger into the gills to break its neck. And the crooked cock of the head relative to the body. I remember Grace throwing herself on the bed, exactly how she pouts when she says I'm stupid, how thin she is, her body straight as a fish. I can see her now. The sea has its own light, a blink of brightness. There is always sea in the light of an island. She lies on her bed in our house, constructing her dilemmas. Richard and Mother and Em are downstairs. Richard's boat is anchored in the bay.

Whales are following the tide.

Seals are moaning.

The stones face the ocean impassively, never suspecting that the ocean will win.

It is that time.

Grace

My sister Emily died. She fell from the watchtower. She was scrambling on the stones of the wall.

Jeannie said that Em had taken to following her, that she was always in and out of the tower.

Later the coroner would say that she had injured herself on the way down, that her back was broken too. Richard Wood and my father made the story straight for him. He praised their clear concise evidence and expressed his sympathy with the family. A childhood accident, he said. He quoted the Bible. They know not what they do. They never asked me. At that time I had other ideas, though I came to believe their story.

I was the one who found her. I should have been taking care of her. But I knew where to look. I brought her ashore. Richard Wood was not there. My mother waited at the pier. I carried Em to her and gave the child into her hands. Then I pushed the boat into deeper water and started the Seagull. I went for the doctor and the lifeboat and I phoned Tiraneering from the public box above Rally Pier. They got to the island before me.

My mother wanted to bury the child there but it was against the law.

Laws of interment are ancient instruments. They are designed
to prevent contagion, disease, and theft. They only *appear* to be
concerned with dignity, love, hospitality. In reality a grave is a
piece of property like any other. It is a small piece of land into
which a child is put. It has a stone with the child's name. Time
elapsed is recorded. It is a complete archive. It contains flesh and
bone and memory and the parentheses of birth and death. And
in the end, like most property, it is owned by someone other than
the occupant. It is a mortgage on the past.

The coroner pieced together a narrative of her death for us.

We experienced it as a piece of fiction, less credible in fact
because it had no internal order, no structuring principle. We fell
apart. The world fell apart.

But the coroner's inquiry could not touch us.

My memories were useless and, in fact, I was already forget-
ting. It would take me thirty years to remember my part in it. I
could tell how she slept with her nose to my back. How she held
my mother's hand when she was talking to her, looking up at her
face and just holding her hand like a toy. Those things cast no
light on the matter, though he listened to them patiently enough.

My mother remembered. She gave evidence in a tight, hurt
voice, like a frightened child reciting last night's homework. Even
I could see that she was in danger of falling apart, or that she had
already fallen apart and been put together the wrong way. She kept
looking at my father and he nodded and smiled at her.

This is what she said. Em had been with her in the kitchen. It was
teatime. It was my day. Then Em was gone. Where is that notice-box
of a child? And where is Grace? I'll have to go after her. Then she
broke down and cried. The coroner gave her tissues. He seemed to
have a box ready just in case. Perhaps coroners always do.

In time she continued. She told them that she knew something
terrible had happened.

Everyone looked for Em.

I was the one who saw her. I climbed the watchtower wall because it was the highest thing on the island. From the height of the tower I saw her drifting in the submarine currents, among the white and rounded shale from the last cliff fall. She wore blue dungarees and a pink-and-white striped shirt and one blue rubber sneaker. Her hands were outstretched.

She sometimes slept like that too, face down in her bed.

My mother's horror was terrible. I remember very little of it. There was a time when I recalled it all but I found it useless in dealing with her life or my own. Memory is an overrated capacity. It is most useful to those who need to deny things. I remember she was upstairs in bed and my sister Jeannie and I were sitting in the kitchen. There were candles on the table because the electricity cable had failed, as it often did—boats were forever anchoring on it, despite the warning signs. My father and Richard Wood were upstairs. We could hear my mother's voice. It came in rapid stuttering bursts, like a sewing machine. I remember that an earwig walked across the table in front of us. Jeannie pinched it up and held it to the light. I saw its jaws working, its tail bending and straightening, its antennae. Then she dropped it into the candle. It fell into the molten wax and settled quickly down. It drowned. In the morning there was the shadow of the earwig in the cold wax.

My mother's horror was also perfectly reasonable. One of the things we forget is that the world itself is madder than anything our heads can make. How should one remember one's child falling into the sea? Sustaining injuries against the cliff on the way down? After that everything is impossible.

My mother's horror was all-encompassing, all-consuming. It devoured the night and the day, the sun and the moon, God and the future and everything in between. It paralyzed us. It divided us.

Jeannie was crying too. I resented her for doing it. It seemed to me she wanted as always to be the center of attention but nobody paid her any heed. Her tearfulness turned into wailing and then I wanted to choke her. I slapped her once but it only made her worse. Shut up, I said, it's bad enough. Then I said, A pity it wasn't you.

Later, the night before we came out of the island—How long was it between Em's death and our crossing?—I woke to hear running and urgent voices. I stood on the bed to see out the window but I could not see the ground. I ran down and saw that the front door was open. Richard had been sleeping on the kitchen floor. His sleeping bag was empty. I closed the door and went back to bed. My mother's room was empty too. It meant that she had run away again.

After a time I heard the voices coming back. Richard, my father, my mother. They did not go to bed. I fell asleep. In the morning Jeannie said she had been asleep all night but I knew she was not. She was listening too.

Where did my mother go that night? Nobody tells children these things. They hope, maybe they believe, that we sleep through every danger, that childhood is, in fact, a kind of sleepwalk through their adult world. Like someone said that madness is a nightmare in a waking world. And then later they assume we know. As if the simple act of growing up involves absorbing their memories in our own. All that time they were inventing the lie that would ravage my life. I could hear them talking it through. They were talking about me. If I had been older, stronger, wilder, I would have run away. I could swim ashore at high tide. It was the kind of thing I was good at. This is what you'll say to the Guards, they told me, and this is what you'll say at the coroner's court. And then they told me a lie.

Later my father would write a full account of how we came out of the island. How the men on the lifeboat turned their backs out of natural sympathy. One of them was the fisherman who called to tell his stories and who came and went that night that we heard her screaming. He never looked at any of us. It was a wet day. They wore their long sou'westers, their sea boots. They were rough men. They made their living by farming or fishing but they volunteered to save people. They had seen madness before; the hills and the valleys were full of it. They did not want their eyes to say what they saw. They watched the sea and the boat and tended to it with skill and gentleness while my mother wept and raved and my father held her together and we children could not close our eyes. In a sense they had always known this would happen. They had seen her coming ashore on her foraging trips, seen the things she bought, heard her talk. They knew about her wild life in the wilderness of the Atlantic where no woman in her right mind would want to live—in remote places everybody knows everything, or they think of it that way. They saw the kind of children she reared. There's a want there—that was a phrase she picked and brought with her—meaning she was not the full shilling, she'd heard it used. Maybe it was intended for her. Where was Flanagan the cat? Cats can look after themselves and I suppose we always intended to go back for him.

SISTERS

I took the train from Waterloo to Portsmouth Harbour and then the Red Funnel Ferry. I glanced back on the crossing and saw that I was leaving a vast industrial harbor. There were warships at anchor. It was a summer's day and sailing boats were working up with the tide. There was a yawl there. She had a high-clewed Yankee and a staysail. I saw how they trimmed the mizzen hard to keep her nose to it. The man at the tiller wore a blue yachting cap. He was lean and long-limbed. He wore faded red trousers and a blue fisherman's smock. I watched him until he was too far away.

My sister met me at the pierhead. I tried hard to recognize her in the waiting crowd but it was she who picked me out. In five years or six years she had turned into a sullen beauty. In the breakdown of our lives she got my father and I got my mother. She got dark hair and I got fair. She got a perfect complexion and I got freckles. She was sixteen, I was twenty. She opened the trunk for me to put my bag in and left me to close it. Her car was an Anglia. She drove with determination and uncertainty along the waterfront and up the hill past crumbling Victorian summer houses. Then we were among fields and small villages for a time, then a harbor lined with houseboats, elaborate affairs with balconies and patio windows—one had an entire bungalow built on the deck. They were settling gently into their mud berths as the tide fell. There were dismasted dinghies floating outside a clubhouse. Across the water they were closing the huge doors on a boatyard shed. A haze like smoke blurred the outlines of things. The shore blended into the sea and shaded into the scrub trees of the roadside. England looked different down here. London felt like another world, or at least another country.

I asked her about the island.

I told her about our mother, although she didn't ask.

We had to stop on a causeway with the harbor on one side and a bog on the other. I could see she was impatient. A lorry and a tractor were maneuvering to pass each other. I had time to see that this was a tamer sea, the harbor shallow. The distant bleak gleam of mudflats stretched towards the English Channel. There was something closed about the sky. A sullen god lurked in its coverts.

She gets agitated, I said, you remember she used to be like that even before. Remember how she worried about having food in the house that we could use if we got cut off in a storm? She worries about her pills all the time now. She's always double-checking that she's taken them. Sometimes she empties them out on the table and counts what's left and divides it by the number of days since the last prescription. She fusses about small things. It turns to efficiency at work, but at home it's a bit strange—you know, strange.

My sister didn't seem to be listening.

She's still beautiful, that's the amazing thing. I mean, people who don't know her are always impressed. Her eyes are on fire.

Look at that tractor, my sister said, he shouldn't be coming this way.

I said, Mum worries about you.

She put her hand to the horn but didn't blow.

And later we walked a bridle path that led along the backs of gardens and through a beech wood. It was Beatrix Potter and Jane Austen and all the clichés between. We came to a beach. My sister said the stones were chalk flints, Tertiary flints, and quartz pebbles, all rolled round by the sea a million years ago. But there were also fragments of ironstone, sarsenstone, lydianstone, hornstone.

She made them sound like a poem in some unknown language. I saw that she loved stones in a way that she could never love anything else. Until now I had only known London. My wilderness was London Fields or maybe Highgate Cemetery, one of Mother's favorites, or Abney Park, where the founder of the Salvation Army was buried. Jeannie held my hand. There was something childlike about her. I was glad of the warmth. Her hand was small but her fingers were hard and strong. Daddy encouraged her geology and mineralogy, she said. I tried that the other way 'round. Daddy encouraged my psychology. It didn't work. I was jealous, I knew that. I was not a fool. He brought her books. When he was traveling he always thought of her. She was allowed to search his bags. She was allowed to find things. Sometimes he brought stones. She had a piece of alabaster from Italy, a banded agate from Greece, and a moss agate from America. He hides things from me, she said. I found the alabaster in the lining of his old leather bag. It's a game we play.

This is my favorite place, she said. Nobody comes here. I sit in that tree and watch the ships.

What is it like living with Daddy?

He takes care of me. Daddy is the caring type.

Do you remember before?

Daddy says not to go over things. Think of the present, he says. Concentrate on what's happening around you.

She looked around.

The raised beach is still here, she said. It's under the turf. It runs all along this side.

She pointed at a line of shells and gravel.

There's a shell midden, she said. Iron Age, I think.

What does he say about me? Daddy.

He says you're the brilliant one. You'll go far. He says no one ever knows what's going on inside your head. You're the genius and I'm the beauty. Would you give me a hug?

She moved towards me.

Please, she said.

I put my arms around her. Already she was taller than me. My head was against her breast. She put her arms around my shoulders and I put mine around her waist. The long-legged fly and the stone. I don't know how long we stayed like that. Did we glisten like enamel, mica, oil? From a ship in the channel we must have looked permanent, a realist sculpture on the shore, depicting loss, disaster, exile. A mother and child. A sailor and his lass. But it would have been a lie. After a time she patted me on the head as you would pat a child. We're still sisters, she said. Then she stepped away and turned her back on me.

LOVERS

We are fossil hunting at Undercliff beach. It's a September afternoon after school. The sea is a mirror that stretches as far as the horizon. We've walked miles. He was always one for endurance. He wears shorts, a pale yellow shirt, and a pair of battered rubber sneakers. We have a bottle of Robinson's Lemon Barley Water and a wax paper packet of ham sandwiches.

We sit down to examine our only find, a tiny ammonite from the London Clay, solitary in my canvas bag. Still, it is beautiful, coppery, fractured, abstract.

You know, he says, what I love is the imperfections; perfection is a dangerous myth, what we need to love is our immanence, not our possibilities.

I know what he means although I don't know what immanence is—it doesn't seem necessary to the thought. Saying *immanence* means he's treating me as an equal. I like that.

He ignores me. He closes his eyes for a time. When he opens them he indicates the cliffs at our back. Tell me about this place, he says.

So I tell him the story of the chalk and mud that is the island; I know the story well. He lies back, closes his eyes, and listens. Even that lying back is accomplished like a deliberate gesture, an unfolding of the body in equilibrium. I have always known this grace. It's part of the landscape of my childhood, as natural as a tree moving in the wind. His body straightens as smoothly as one might open a fist and straighten a hand. His lean face and clear eyes, then the long pale lashes. Now I can look at his face, now that he can't see me. I try to memorize it. The downy hair around his lips, almost like a girl's. In the steely light I see it. And a tiny scar near his left eye, so smooth I feel I could rub it away with my finger.

It's a dream—the flat sea, the hot sand, the canvas bag of tools, and the single burnished ammonite. The story of the rock, the clay, the sand, told in millions of years. Sweat on my face, in my armpits, between my breasts and my legs. The humidity is rising. Over on the French side of the channel I can see cumulus building into giant anvils. As I talk I learn something new and it is this: that two people could commit any enormity and it wouldn't alter the long history of stone by as much as a micron. On this day in the four-and-half-billion-year existence of the Earth I could have exactly what I want, what I had always wanted, and afterwards the universe would be exactly the same without waste, without imbalance. So when I see that he's asleep I bend down and put my mouth close to his. I am careful not to touch. I am so close I can almost feel my own shadow.

He wakes. I draw back. I feel my face redden. I try to look away.

Then he puts his arms around me and pulls me down. Later he says that he did it because he didn't want to hurt me, he didn't want me to feel rejected. But it doesn't feel like that.

First there is the kiss. Everything is rougher than I expected. By the time he feels for my breast I am beyond caring, beyond doing, beyond resistance, beyond common sense. I've fallen for sex, fallen into sex, I'm falling in sex.

He's almost weightless. When he enters me it hurts and my pain belongs to the subterranean world, primitive as the clay. His body is slacker than I expected; a small paunch begins at his waist and settles in a downward parabola to his groin. His pubic hair is red. His penis is a surprise although I had imagined what they would feel like, read about them, seen them represented on toilet walls and magazines. I didn't see it before he entered me, but afterwards it is small and sticky and amusing. I want to touch it but I don't dare. I don't know the etiquette. He is twenty or more years older than me. This is sex.

He rolls sideways onto the sand.

Oh god, he says.

I think it sounds like anguish. I don't care. I find I'm holding my breath. I release it slowly. Sex, I tell myself. I've had it. Sex. Somewhere in a disconnected but synchronous life, a point from which I can view myself to advantage and still belong, I am amused. There I am lying in the sand, full of semen. This is sex. I've had sex. There are fossils everywhere. I'm marveling and silently laughing. I'm inwardly celebrating and at the same time reverent. Sex.

I lie there with my legs spread, my shirt pulled down awkwardly. The old bag of tools is beside my head. I can almost sense the numinous reality of the ammonite. I'm sore but not as much as I had imagined. I've been learning things from magazines, though they haven't prepared me for the fullness, the experience of being ridden, of his final explosive stop. The terror is pleasure. There isn't enough of it. I want it again. I want to be able to experience each part of it distinctly, not as a single astonishing mass. Sex. It just happened. I've had it.

We talk seriously once we've arranged our clothes again. The clouds have come from France and the sky is lowering. We're at the upper extent of the sand and there are scars of grey clay like the broken crust of the world. First of all there are apologies I don't want. Then there are the people we can't tell. My stepmother would be shocked. She might go to the police. I think the police thing is laughable. And I actually laugh. He doesn't. He is a guest, he has broken the most fundamental rules, if there is a baby he would acknowledge it, of course, he would not run away from his responsibilities—all that primitive nonsense. He sits with his knees doubled up under his chin, his arms wrapped around them. He looks like a miserable midget. I want to say to him that this is not 1876, that I know what I'm doing, that I'm not a child, that this is the age of liberation. I've read articles in which people say these things.

I'm so sorry, he keeps saying, I'm not good at self-control.

In the end, child that I am, I laugh in his face.

Do it to me again, I say as if to prove that I know what I'm doing. I begin to unbutton my shorts.

Oh no, he says, oh no, my girl, I'm not falling for it again.

He looks along the beach.

He stands up suddenly. He walks towards the water, which is coming in our direction. I know this part of the beach can get cut off at spring tide, people have been rescued here. I think about being cut off for six hours or so with him. He picks up one piece of shingle after another and launches them into the water. Some skip on the surface for a while before they go down. I watch him. I feel cool and powerful. When he turns around again he stares silently at me for about ten seconds. Then he begins walking back the way we came. When I get up to follow him I feel where he's been. The soreness is a peculiar pleasure, a memento. A child no more, it says.

HONEYMOON PHOTOGRAPH

We had a room that opened into an orange garden. It was February and a cold wind was blowing from the Apennines and beyond that from the mountains of Greece. They called it the Grecale.

It was a surprise to us.

We had imagined a warmer place. Nevertheless I fell in love with it. Perhaps I am drawn to coldness. In time I would learn Italian, translate from Italian, even think about buying a small house in the country somewhere. I never did, of course. I knew too much about small houses.

It was so cold that on our first day we went into town and bought warm underwear and socks. In the haberdashery, the man knew exactly what we wanted. He brought a stepladder and reached down boxes from the highest row, the just-in-case shelves. Everything came in tissue paper.

The oranges were as cold as stones but they were the brightest thing—winter's lights. We walked a lot. I loved it, Bill did not. He was impatient with everything, he thought the people unreliable, the food too oily and sloppy, but when we closed the door on the orange garden and turned out the lights he was as happy as a child. I might have been worried by his cunning sensuality, the perfection of his pleasure. I was not much good at sex, but he didn't care. He created my body. He imagined my arousal and my satisfaction and they happened as he imagined. It may have been his experience in television that gave him this power. I was grateful for it, anyway. It gave me time to learn both pretense and pleasure. I was happily full of him, rosy-cheeked at dinner, pale at breakfast. The man behind the desk approved—we called him Antonio. Bill named him one night. Naked and flabby in the cold light from the one overhead bulb, he danced and sang:

Her old hurdy-gurdy
All day she'd parade
And this she would sing
To the tunes that it played

Oh! Oh! Antonio, he's gone away
Left me alone-ee-o, all on my own-ee-o
I want to meet him with his new sweetheart
Then up will go Antonio and his ice cream cart

Bill's repertoire of ridiculous songs is vast. I'll say one thing for old Bill, he can make me laugh. He did the hurdy-gurdy handle with his prick and the ice cream cart going up was executed with panache, turning his back to me and flipping his backside in the air like a cancan dancer.

Antonio wore beautiful shirts, whiter than white, in the words of the advertisements. They seemed to glow against his skin. He was always perfectly groomed; he even shaved again in the afternoon. The girl who served us our coffee looked at us with longing. We thought she was the reason he shaved so often. She had no ring.

It was a time when many people did not own cameras. Our only honeymoon photograph was taken by Antonio on his Brownie box camera. He stood back under the orange trees, stooped over the reflex lens, the strap around his neck. Two eyes, one big, one small, watched us from the box. When he pressed on the arm the shutter opened and we saw the big eye wink briefly. There we are in the unnatural and slightly garish Kodacolor, fading now, clearly happy and in love. I don't think the image is a lie. We are seated at the table where we always took our breakfast. It was just outside the dining room of the hotel, sheltered by two walls from the Grecale that blew in the trees overhead. The morning sun reached in there after a certain hour, its blessed warmth on our faces. I'm wearing a sweater and green flares. My legs are crossed under the table, feet in leather sandals. Bill is in shirtsleeves. There is coffee and bread and a bowl of fruit on the table. A white linen tablecloth. The whiteness of the walls and the fabric impresses itself rather too much. Our faces are milky by comparison. I'm laughing, Bill is making a face.

Antonio posted the print to us. No one would do it now. His real name was Enzo, it turned out. Enzo Muratore. I still have the postcard he enclosed with it. It was a photograph of Vesuvius.

THE MOUNTAIN ROAD

James Casey drove off the top of Rally Pier. His two daughters were in the back seat. The tide here falls out through the islands and away west. It runs at a knot, sometimes a knot and a half, at springs. Listen and you will hear it in the stones. This is the song of lonely places. The car moved a little sideways as it sank. And afterwards great gulps of air escaped but made no sound. I know these things, not because I saw them but because they must have happened. The sky is settling over Rally and the hills. It is the color of limestone, a great cap on the country. Ten miles out the sky is blue.

I heard it on local radio, suicide at Rally Pier. I knew who it was.

You cannot see the pier from my house. I got up and put my jeans and sweater on and climbed the hill behind the house, through heather and stone, to where I could look down. Bees sang in the air. Watery sunshine filtered through thin clouds. When I turned after ten minutes of climbing, the whole bay lay before me, the islands in their pools of stillness, the headlands like crude fingers, boats out beyond Castle Island pair-trawling a mile or more apart but connected forever by cables attached to the wings of a giant net. James was on the boats once. He it was who explained all that to me. I saw the police tape on the pier head, a tiny yellowness that was not there before. If he left a note, what did it say? Suddenly the song came into my head. "Dónal Óg." Even as the first words came I knew what it meant for me. You took the east from me and you took the west from me and great is my fear that you took God from me.

When the song was finished with me I walked back down home. I was accustomed to think of it like that—not that I stopped singing but that the song was finished with me. I made up the bed with fresh sheets and put the soiled ones in the washing machine. I washed out the floor of the bathroom. Why do we do these things when we are bereft? Then I had a shower and put on dark clothes. I got out the bicycle and pumped up the leaking tire. My father had shown me how to mend punctures but I could not remember now. I still have the same puncture repair kit, a tin box, but now I keep hash in it.

Then I wheeled the bicycle down to the gate and onto the road and faced the hill to the house where the dead girls lay.

They closed the door against me when they saw me turn the bend. Cousins make these decisions, but I leaned my bicycle against the wall and knocked and then they had to let me in. Perhaps it was inevitable anyway. People around here do not shut their neighbors out. They showed me into the front room where the two girls lay in open coffins. Three older women sat by them. I did not recognize them. Aunts, most probably. They had their beads in their hands. I did not bless myself. I go to neither church nor chapel and they all know it. I stood for a long time looking down on the faces. When old people go, death eases their pain and their faces relax into a shapeless wax model of someone very like them. People say they look happy, but mostly they look plastic. But when a child dies it is the perpetuation of a certain model of perfect beauty. People would say the girls looked like angels. There was no trace of the sea on them, no sign of the panic and fear that bubbled through the ground-up sleeping tablets that their father had fed them for breakfast yesterday morning. According to local radio. His own prescription. He had not been sleeping for months.

When I stopped looking I shook hands with each of the aunts.

Nobody said anything. I went out of the room and found the cousins waiting in the corridor. I asked for Helen and was told she was lying down. The doctor was calling regularly all day. She was on tablets for her nerves. She was very low. I was about to ask them to pass on my sympathy when a door opened upstairs. It was Helen herself. She called to know who was there. It's your neighbor, one of the cousins said. She could not bring herself to name me.

Helen came unsteadily down the stairs.

Her hair was flat and moist. She was wearing the kind of clothes she might have gone to mass in, a formal blouse and a straight grey skirt, but she had no tights on. Her bare feet looked vulnerable and childish. She stepped deliberately, stretching so that at each tread of the stairs she stood on the ball of her foot like a dancer. She came down like someone in a trance. I think we all wondered if she knew who she was coming down for. And if she did, what was she going to say.

Cáit, she said, is it yourself? Thank you for coming.

Her eyes were flat, too. There was no light in them.

I'm sorry for your trouble, I said, taking her hand. I held the hand tightly as if the pressure could convey something in itself.

Helen shook her head.

Why did he do it? she said. Even if he went himself. But the girls . . .

Helen, will I make you a cup of tea?

One of the cousins said that. She was by Helen's side now, she would like to take her arm and lead her into the kitchen. They did not want her going into the front room and starting the wailing and the cursing all over again. Jesus, Mary, and Joseph, it would terrify you to hear the things she said. And here she was now talking to Cáit Deane like nothing happened at all.

There was cake and several kinds of bread and honey and tea and coffee and a bottle of the hard stuff and stout and beer. The house was provided against a famine. They'd need it all by and by. This is the way things go at funerals.

He always spoke well of you, Helen said.

We were childhood sweethearts, I said.

He always said you should have trained professionally. He said you had a great voice.

I shrugged. I heard this kind of thing from time to time.

He said it was a pity what happened to you.

I felt my shoulders straighten. I was fond of him, I said, everybody was.

He said you had terrible bitterness in you.

I moved towards the door but there was a cousin in the way. Excuse me, I said. The cousin did not move. She had her arms folded. She was smiling.

He said you were your own worst enemy.

I turned on her. Well, he was wrong there, I said. I have plenty of enemies.

Helen Casey closed her eyes. The only thing my husband was wrong about was that he took my two beautiful daughters with him. If he went on his own nobody would have a word to say against him. But now he cut himself off from everything. Even our prayers. If that man is burning in hell, it's all the same to me. I hope he is. He'll never see my girls again, for they're not in hell. And the time will come when you'll join him and no one will be sorry for that either.

One of the cousins crossed herself and muttered under her breath. Jesus, Mary, and Joseph.

The doorkeeper unfolded her arms suddenly and stepped aside. I opened the door. I was taken by surprise to find the priest outside preparing to knock.

Oh, he said.

Excuse me, Father.

I pushed past him. I noticed that the tire was sinking again; it would need pumping, but I could not do it here. I turned it to face away from the house. People say I'm cold. A coldhearted bitch, some of them say. They say such things. The priest was watching me. He was smiling. The new man in the parish, most likely he did not know who I was. They'd fill him in on the details in the front room with the two dead girls and the old women with their beads. The cousins would know everything. It was how crows always knew there was bread out. First came a single bird, a scout. There was always one. Then they gather. Before long they're fighting each other over crusts. You can knock fun out of watching them and their comical battles in the back yard. But the minute you put the bread out, one of them turns up to check it out and the others follow soon enough. If you dropped dead on your own lawn they'd be down for your eyes.

I swung onto my bicycle and launched myself down the tarmac drive and out onto the road and I turned for the hill down home but that was not where I was going.

I met the car at the place where the road was falling into the valley. There was no question of slipping past. I braked hard and dragged my foot along the road. By the time I stopped I was by the driver's door and there was a drop of a hundred feet on my left-hand side. He rolled the window down. It was James's brother Johnny.

You'd think the council would shore that up, he said.

The crows are gathering.

He nodded.

The priest was at the door.

He nodded again. He looked at me silently for a moment, then he said, He could have asked for help, Cáit. You'd have helped him, wouldn't you? I would any day. All he had to do was ask.

Johnny, I said, you know very well I was the last one he'd turn to. And the last one who could help him. And anyway, there is no help.

You could but you would not.

No, I said, I just could not. You know that very well.

Do you know what, Cáit Deane?

I probably do, Johnny.

He looked at me, frustrated. You were always the same. You're too sharp for around here.

I shrugged.

My brother James, he said, you destroyed him.

He destroyed himself. I didn't drive him down to the pier.

Why did he do it if not for you? You took him. You took him and you wouldn't keep him and then you left him. Why else would he do it?

I got my foot on the pedal again and faced down the hill.

Spite, I said. He was always spiteful, like a spoiled child.

I launched myself forward and went clear of the car. In a moment I was past the subsiding section. Fuchsia speckled the roadsides with their first bloody skirts. In the valley the last of the whitethorn blossom. The river at the very bottom gleaming like concrete in a field of bog iris. And ahead was the bay and its islands and the vast intolerant ocean.

I chained the bicycle to the stop sign outside the funeral home. The street was a long one that ran into a steep hill; the funeral home, the graveyard, and the church were all at the top of the hill so that the dead could look down on the town, and the townspeople when they looked up from the pavement saw death looming like a public monument to their future. People joked that it was the only town in Ireland where you had to climb up to your grave. To make matters worse, the funeral home was owned by the Hill family. There were several Hills in the parish and naturally the funeral home was called the Hilton. They say that the only people making money out of the economic crash were accountants and funeral directors. Even the bankrupt had to be buried by somebody. At the door in a plastic frame was a poster with a picture of an anorexic bonsai plant and the words: Our promise to you, Phone ANY TIME, day or night, You will NEVER get an answering machine.

Funeral homes are always cold. There were pine benches in lines like a church. They had been varnished recently and there was that heady smell. It reminded me of my father's boat, the wheelhouse brightwork newly touched up. It was the smell of childhood.

James Casey lay in a plain wooden box at the top of the room. I could see immediately that the brass handles were fake. Someone had examined a funeral menu and ticked *cheap*. I went to look down on him. I thought I had nothing to say but when I was standing there I had plenty.

You stupid bastard, I said, you stupid murdering fucking bastard.

There was more like that. I surprised myself with the flow of anger, the dam-burst of fury. After a time I stopped because I was afraid I was going to attack the corpse. And then I thought I might have been shouting. No one came; perhaps funeral directors and their secretaries are used to angry mourners. I stepped back and found my calf touching a bench. I sat down.

They'll all blame me, I told him. They already blame me.

Then I cried.

James Casey looked tranquil and unperturbed. In real life he was never like that. After a time I got up. I looked down at him. His eyes were stitched closed because when he was pulled from the sodden car of course they were open. They are not very expert in our part of the world; I could see the stitches here and there. The funeral director knows from experience that the eyes of dead people do not express emotion but he knows that his clients would see fear in them. Nobody wants to look a dead man in the eye. It's bad for business.

Fuck you, I said.

I turned on my heel and walked out. A tiny sigh escaped when I closed the door, like the seal opening on an airtight jar. My bicycle lay on the ground in its chains. They knifed the tires while I was with James. I was not going to give them the satisfaction of watching me wheel it down the street. I was going to leave it where I found it. Do not slouch, my mother used to say, stand up straight, put your shoulders back. But I slouched just the same. How many years since I first loved James Casey? I pulled my shoulders back but I kept my eyes on the ground. The thought that I had done something unforgivable was always there in the dark. Things come back in the long run, the way lost things are revealed by the lowest tides: old shipwrecks, old pots, the ruined moorings that once held steadfastly to trawlers or pleasure boats. There are no secrets around here.

THE LAST ISLAND

1

The little island ferry came through the entrance and immediately began to slow down. She made a slight turn about three
hundred meters out and dropped anchor. Then she pulled against
the anchor chain and that resistance turned her so that the stern
was towards the land. It was a graceful and gallant maneuver, a
curtsy. There are three islands, he told me on the phone, take care
that you don't fall asleep in the ferry or you'll end up visiting all
three in turn. It was late morning and the ferry was quiet. I could
really have slept to the beat of the engine and the sea.

He met me at the port captain's office. I scarcely recognized
him. He had a grey beard and his hair was white as Formica.

He drove me up through the narrow lanes, crazy with Fiat
Puntos and motor scooters and pedestrians who shrank away
from the traffic, and we came to a place where he could park his
car. We went in at a gate and there was the garden and the house.
It was not what I expected.

He brought me upstairs and showed me a room. Come down
when you're ready, he said, and we'll have a drop of wine.

There were two windows. In the distance was the sea, the haze of the mainland, the old broken back of Vesuvius. That old mountain had done enough damage in its time.

The house was plainer, older than I thought it would be. It was emptier, too. Quieter. That would change when the others came. It was his seventieth birthday. The road below my window was narrow and across the way there was a lemon grove, a single old kitchen chair in the shade. An old woman walked through it carrying a watering can and a hoe. She wore a straw hat. Among the distant gardens, the cicadas were bitter about the heat. The geckos waited for evening. They looked on human existence as a temporary interruption in the hegemony of stone. They stopped for hours in one place and then on some geodetic sign shifted like a clockwork toy. There was no difference between the new station and the old, no difference in light or air, no obvious reason for change. At night they cavorted after insects and made weird upside-down leaps onto cornices or street lamps.

The table stood under a square frame over which the vines crossed. In clusters the pale grapes caught shafts of sunlight. The shade was delicious. A wooden ladder stood against the frame at one side. The table was of some kind of wood too, rough-hewn enough, a country table, but the chairs were plastic. He brought a tray with two glasses of wine, some olives, some bread. I said that all gardens are magical.

Yes. They all have one. The island of gardens.

He made a gesture that was intended to encompass everything.

There's an old lady across the street from my bedroom watering her vegetables.

They do that. There's never enough rain.

I was glad to have seen her. The earth is important still.

He nodded. He agreed with that.

So tell me about you, he said. How are you? How are you faring?

Without ever having thought of the idea before I said, I'm shipwrecked.

He laughed. Then he frowned. Bill?

Bill, yes.

So how are you managing it?

I took a deep breath. I said I was coping but things were coming to a head.

And if you don't mind, I don't like talking about it.

As you wish.

Something lapidary in the light, every shadow edged, exact, more itself than before. He put his hand on the nape of my neck. It fitted there. I had the feeling that he too was on the verge of revelation but that he turned away at the very last.

Instead he said, Come and look at Salvatore's rabbits.

He was up again, leaving the wine and food. He looked unsettled. There was something nervous and disturbing about him. He led me out under the grapes. There were walls, shallow steps that led nowhere, wisteria, bougainvillea trailing everywhere, the thick tonguey leaves of the magnolia, the grapes, the lemon trees, the chipped statue of an armless Venus surrounded by cactus—an installation, he told me, one of Serena's, the statue and the cactus had to be read together, the whole situation a totality. He didn't sound convinced.

Only the blue sky suggested that there was a world beyond. So this was his new island, his walled paradise. Once there was sea, now there was stone. He was always longing to be outside.

We went down to where the vines spiraled onto old branches slung between posts and tied with rags. Salvatore—their neighbor who looked after the house when they traveled—kept them and had the grapes. He made wine with them. It had to be drunk young, a small wine like all the locals, but quite good. Then in a slatted shade there was a stone oven big enough almost to get my shoulders into. Again, Salvatore built it. The Centane stone was famously hard. Then an orchard of stunted lemon and orange trees. The fruits were last year's crop and not good for eating; they had been on the tree over winter and the cold spring winds dried them out, and the new fruit was small and hard and green still.

Through a gap in the wall he brought me to where his neighbor kept rabbits and hens in cages.

He looked at me ruefully. They really are almost self-sufficient, the islanders. They have to be.

Food that travels farther than the length of a parish isn't worth eating?

He started. I could see he was trying to remember. So many books, how could he remember one line.

He said: It's a funny thing, people quoting your own work back at you.

I know.

I don't like it.

There were pumpkins growing in the floor of a half-finished house and basil plants and rosemary, a fig tree with tiny hard fruits and a twisted olive tree whose trunk had split in two maybe a hundred years before; the ghost of the second half seemed necessary to sustain its precarious balance.

It was the kind of garden that could be found in any house on the island that had the space, he said, as all the older ones did. Everybody grew their own food, if they could. But it was all changing now. They have a saying, *Stavamo meglio quando stavamo peggio.* We were better when we were worse.

He collected half a dozen eggs and I made a basin of my shirt and he put them into it. And standing there, with a shirtful of eggs, and looking at him, I said, Once upon a time I wanted to kill you.

He stared at me. He didn't say anything. He still held an egg in each hand. There were four in my shirt. If, for example, he had embraced me suddenly we would have broken everything.

I never bother to remember dreams. Despite my training, or perhaps because of it, I don't really believe in them. They have always seemed to me to be essentially trivial, housekeeping for the brain or at best an exercise in poetics. But that first night on the island I dreamed that I was looking in the windows of a car and it was like looking into a fish tank. My father was there, floating like an astronaut or a baby in a womb. The light was green and uncertain. His head was too big and his eyes were pearlescent and unresponsive. He might have been blind like a puppy. He was wearing the ochre-colored canvas trousers that he used to wear when we were children; it was wet and the thinness of his legs showed through. Why had his legs become so thin? His arms, too. I felt a surge of terrible pity. It came to me that the glass would not break because of the pressure—I had seen something to that effect in a film or television program, people trying to break out of a car underwater—so I simply looked on as he floated. He moved with wonderful grace, in slow motion, without any sign of pain or fear. I knew, as I watched, that I should be happy for him. If I broke the glass he would wash out into our world and things would begin again. But, in fact, when the first pity vanished it was replaced by revulsion and anger. I was the one who felt pain, who felt suffocated. I was drowning for him. I had to break the glass or die. I began to look for a weapon.

I got up and stood at my window.

2

When I visited my sister, she lived with my father. She got him and I got my poor mad mother. The train from Waterloo to Portsmouth Harbour and the Red Funnel Ferry to the island. She too was at the pierhead. I slept in a small room at the top of the house. There too I was looking out on the garden. The air was sliced by swallows. The evenings were heavy with valerian and mock orange.

The next room was my father's office. I thought it would be his bedroom. There was a large locked filing cabinet. A clock that told the time in New York, London, and Tokyo. A mahogany bookcase that mostly contained his own books in different editions and languages. The center of the room was taken up by a partner's desk with a chair at both sides. On its vast gleaming surface there was a Remington typewriter and a block of blank paper; opposite them, in front of the second chair, a typescript. I listened for any sounds in the house or garden but there were none.

He was writing about my mother. I think my mother's appearances in his books represented for her absolute truths about her life and personality. They came swift as judgment and struck her to the bone. This other self that we never express. They were, first of all, ideal forms of her life, potential existences that she always failed to realize. They were myths of happiness and self-sufficiency. Then there were tales of her madness fixed forever in words not of her choosing. They were his narrative of how she fell from grace: her lapses, her comical aporia, her diatonic weeping, her infidelity. She saw herself. She understood that she was an ex-angel, a pitiful fallen creature with a broken wing. She saw too that he was her imprisoned narrator. His readers would long for his release. Now he was beginning again. The starting point was different. This was memoir.

One paragraph shocked me: "Nevertheless, and despite my advice, Jane persisted in her belief that the children should have tomatoes in summertime to eat with their salads. To achieve this impossible task she set about buying a glasshouse in bits and pieces, an old wooden glasshouse that was once attached to the southern wall of a Victorian cottage about twenty miles away on the mainland. She had it imported to our island, panel by panel, on the post boat which could spare the time in winter to call at our pier but which was too busy in the summer."

I didn't remember any glasshouse.

Chapter two was titled "The Mental: Cork." Now I saw that what he had done was turn her madness into a story and the story had made everything that happened inevitable and that inevitability absolved us all, but most of all, him. I could see why he had taken so many years to write it. It would be a difficult book.

I had seen her in that hospital. They called it The Red Brick and sometimes The Mental. There were old people everywhere. They were doing nothing. My mother was sitting in a glassed-in porch with a lot of others. Their chairs were against the wall. They were facing outwards to the winter sun. She did not look out of place. She said nothing for a long time. Then she cried. She called me Child of Grace. It was an old joke of hers. When I heard it I knew she was the same person now as before and I tried to think how I could get her out. I had dreams of organizing her escape. Child of Grace, she said, will I tell you a secret? But a nurse came and I never heard the secret. I wasn't sure I wanted to hear it. But at that moment, I think, there began in me the fascination with the hurt mind. I wanted to cure it. I was convinced it could be done.

When I went to boarding school I was relieved. Because I could do nothing I felt the responsibility was no longer mine. Nothing could be as terrible as watching your mother being mad. But at night I thought about her. I could not stop wondering what it was like to be mad among madwomen, to be in a madhouse, to be hurt, to believe that you had caused the death of your own child, or neglected to save her, to have no way back, to always have that absence, that little nose between your shoulder blades, to be able to feel the steady breathing, or whatever recollection most troubled her, and to know that it was only madness, that the child was dead. The child is dead. There are few worse sentences in the English language.

What I wanted most of all was to burn it. What I did was take the typescript and replace it with the same thickness of blank paper. I arranged the paper carefully so no one would know. I left the room and closed the door. I put it in my vanity bag and went back to London and my studies. Also in my baggage was a consciousness of all that my textbooks had to say about fathers and daughters, Carl Jung and his Electra complex and all the rest of it. We travel in two boats always, two cars, two trains; in one a person passes seas and roads and the back doors of other people's houses. In the other we navigate inhospitable seas and struggle with impossible creatures of the mind. I had chosen to make the second voyage my profession, but professional or not, I traveled in that same boat. My journey home was an agony of hurt and shame and fear; I was a terrified passenger, an exile to myself, a lonely child inside a university student.

I recalled everything. That corner of Ireland that faces the Atlantic. An island off the coast of an island on the edge of Europe. Those cold seas, green and grey and black and white, the wailing of seabirds, the barking of seals, the sudden sigh of a whale breaching, my father's absence, my mother and her lover and all the jealousies and trivial rivalries that animate childhood. I remembered the time my sister Em died. I remembered every detail of that black day from breakfast to catastrophe and the night that followed.

In that I was like my mother.

My sister drove me to the boat. I remember when she was a little girl she had a book called *Aurora the Sleeping Beauty*; it was a coloring book based on the Walt Disney motion picture. And in it Princess Aurora became Briar Rose. I remember her sitting in the window coloring the outlines. There is always something extra in the light of an island. It is the presence of the sea, like living in a world where there is always a mirror just out of sight.

As I left the island the bins at Portsmouth Pier were full to overflow and so I held on to the manuscript until Waterloo. People stared at me on the train. Since then, in a life of research and fitful practice as a psychologist, I have met many weeping girls. They weep for the imaginary as much as the real, or for the imagined real. Their sorrow is their own and cannot be taken from them. And I husbanded mine against the sympathy of strangers. I nursed my grief.

It was the commonplace book of Mother's madness. My father only knew the beginning, but I saw it right through to the end. That obstinate hurt that diverted her life. It made a fanatic of her. It made her immovable. It made her irretrievably other. She was still my mother. It was impossible. Yeats wrote: Hearts with one

purpose alone / Through summer and winter, seem / Enchanted
to a stone / To trouble the living stream.

   That was her.

3

There were two coffee cups, a little jug of boiled milk and an espresso pot, a copy of yesterday's *Telegraph* (it's all they get here) folded to the crossword. The curdled skin on the milk like a drift of burnt plastic. There was a little bowl of white butter, already losing its shape in the heat, a plate of bread, two pieces of pastry. They were called *lingua di bue*, he said, which means ox tongue. They were a specialty of the place. They looked lascivious enough. We sat down to breakfast. I had seen photographs of him sitting here. I remember one page-length feature; the theme was, Radical critic finds peace at last.

He looked deflated, like a balloon that had cooled, and I thought there was a pallor in his tan, something chemical almost, and a dry slack skin.

Are you all right?

Yes, I'm all right, I'm fine, I'm not sleeping well that's all.

Is there something wrong?

Old age has laid her hand on me. Do you know the song? Frank Harte.

Go on, Grace, ask him now, I thought. There's no time like the present. I took a deep breath, but he spoke first.

What you said yesterday, about wanting to kill me . . .

Tell me about your life here, I said. He looked relieved.

So he told me things about the island instead of himself. That it was formed in the eruptions of the Phlegrean Fields, twelve thousand years ago, and is really no more than the joined rims of three volcano craters. He said it was the most densely populated rural area in the world; that the walled village at the southern end used to contain a penitentiary, now a community center, and that consequently it was a closed island until 1967 and you needed a *permesso* just to land, and that it was one of the places that Mussolini exiled Communists to; that the architecture of the houses was remarkable and unique, more Africa than Europe; that the dialect was impenetrable.

It was a hollow kind of knowledge, I saw, a tourist's précis. It told me nothing.

A language is a world, I said, the unconscious is a language without a grammar. You'll never belong here, you'll never understand these people though you may think you can. You can never experience things the way they do. You can never dream their dreams. You can't even feel the same sun on your face. You'll always be a stranger.

I know, he said, I always have been. And you?

There was a ticking sound in the garden but everything was still. I knew that whatever happened now had already happened before, that every moment had its double, that in fact every moment was dual, containing both directions, both positive and negative, yes and no, that everything had both happened and not happened. It was true I had never felt at home, but I didn't want him to know, him of all people. I wanted him to feel homeless. I wanted him to believe that we all had anchors and he was the restless one, drifting through our moorings, alone. Unbidden a line from his book came to me. How did it return after all these years of repression? He wrote: Jane was faithful to nothing and no one except place; not men, not hope, not dreams, but to an island.

Once there was an island, I said. You weren't there.

I meant we had a home once. We had lost it, but it was there in memory. It was our home, not his.

But he shrugged. All my life you've been shrugging me off, Father. But not anymore. There's no stepping off this island where you find yourself in the end. You've had your day.

You imagined that, he said, you were an exile, we all were, except maybe Jane.

On a wire that ran from a pole to the roof of the house I saw a sparrow with its wings slightly open. All my childhood he was the one who put us in words. He had the copyright of our most private thoughts. Because he owned our utterance we performed it. In the book that never was he said my mother was a careless woman who brought her children up like animals. He wrote that she was a big-boned, handsome woman, generous in everything, gentle in nothing; copious, unpredictable, like a happening in nature, a storm or a flood or a downpour. It might have been a form of praise unknown to me. She took men when she needed them, he said, and he was one. He never said that she had a brain.

He wrote that a parent never forgives herself for the death of a child. There was a long passage about blamelessness that was really about blame. He forgave her but she was lost forever in the interstices of guilt and desire. His forgiveness could not pass to her. And there was no return.

Yet I saw that he yearned most of all to be her lover, gliding in on a breeze, anchoring in the lucid water, taking the woman, making the poems. He wanted more than anything to be an itinerant maker, like an old man we used to see beating old copper cylinders into pots and polishing them, who came and went in the country on some calendar of his own imagining. My father was continually handling beautiful things, exquisite phrases and ideas, but they were borrowed. He poisoned them and they passed from hand to hand, elegant but dangerous devices. Slogans, not poems. When my father wanted to talk about remorse it was unbearable; in the book that never was, it was an obscenity, a human organ grafted to a stone, a *pietà* stitched with a bleeding breast. Sitting in the train in the burning waterless landscape of 1976, I remember it exactly, it was on the patch of track between between Guildford and Woking, I saw that he had cut me off from her, that I could never be in her thoughts again, that he had waved his witch's wand and made her an émigré in the islands. He had reduced her voice to a babble. In the book that never was.

His children? He said we only wore clothes when we were told to. We fought like spitting cats. We killed birds and fish. In the nighttime echoing island we prowled and pried and discovered everything. We inherited her casual sexuality. I was beyond help, but my younger sister could be saved. Our mother's madness lay before us. He might have said, Intemperance is naturally punished with diseases. He might have said, What good were eyes to me?

It was a tissue of signs. It was, as always, himself, the book that never was. In a moment, in the sunlight from the high glass roof, in beautiful Waterloo Station, I held his life to be burgled, it was mine to dispose of. All I remember is joy. The bin was full again. I remember there was the bottom half of a dried-up ham sandwich. The yellow of the mustard.

I said, The simple truth is we all hate you.

He smiled. It surprised me. He wore a round-necked T-shirt. When he smiled the scalene muscles hung like ropes from his cheek to his chest. His skin was mottled and cracked. There were purple shadows under his eyes. Only his lips seemed to have become fuller and richer and more sensual with age. They were red now, like a girl's. Only the tip of his nose had not regained its color.

No, he said, you know that's not true. It's what you felt at the time, but you of all people know that the opposite is the case.

I shook my head.

We got over all that.

No, he said again. I gave you a childhood like no other. Jane and I, we created that island, a colony of peace and strength in a world that was about to annihilate itself. You never feared the bomb, like other children. When people elsewhere in the world were building bomb shelters you were swimming in the ocean. You never learned the commodity fetish from television. You were free spirits. You are what you are because of that. It was a gift that few children of your generation were given.

Hippies, I said. What did you give us? Look at us, we're the unhappiest family in the world.

He smiled again. You say that, but you know it's not true. You, of all people, a psychologist, you know exactly what the balance of happiness and unhappiness is.

It's true if I say it's true.

He shook his head. He moved the cup on the table. He looked down and up again.

None of us is a whole person, I said, our hearts are broken.

Child, he said, you have no idea.

I saw that his hand was shaking. He moved the cup again and I saw the slightest tremor. We notice these things, a professional skill, we swimmers in other people's psyches. He was controlling it as best he could. I might have pitied him. At his age pity is the same as love. Or it's enough. It is the end encoded in the beginning. The end of the law of the father.

Why did you never have more children?

He looked away.

I already had two.

Three, I said.

He was silent for a time. Then he looked at me. His eyes were pinched and dry. What was he afraid of? Now, I thought, there will be more lies. But he just turned away.

I walked the island lanes, thinking it through, thinking about him. It meant I didn't have to watch him sulk. I climbed through streets that turned into private roads that forced me to retrace my steps and start again, that wound in and out and then stopped unpredictably, that ended in gates, in doorways, in views over the sea or over the edge. The houses crowded down on each other, built across the path, overhanging me. There were external staircases that climbed sharply or doubled back on each other like tricks of perspective; low roofs that I could look down on from the road, rounded half barrels; doors that seemed to let into cliffs; doors set at an angle to the street or the path; square, round, or trapezoid windows; elaborate shutters, doorknockers, gates. Nothing was straight. Nothing was simple. It was a demented geometry. It was as though the inhabitants had built outwards from some conception of the interior, of the heart or the soul, of the placing of furniture, of opportunities provided by shade or by an irregularity in time or space, as though the world did not exist except as a shell for the inside. I thought, if I could do that with my life. Begin at some space that was my own and build out into the light. But I am walled and roofed by other people's words and the walls grow inwards to fill the space. I am drowning inside.

If I could only touch someone.

There were stagnant pools, a smell of stagnant water and detergent. A smell of other people's food. If I went in I would emerge in someone else's life. I only needed the courage. But when I looked down the narrow corridors I saw old women and men impassive as troglodytes. They belonged to an underworld that stubbornly remained attached by life or love and through which doors and light and gifts passed forward and back.

I walked into evening.

In the lengthening shadows everyone was out-of-doors. People greeted each other as though they had not met in years. It was a parable of concord. So many people lived here on this little heap of black and pumice stone that if they did not meet for a day they considered each other lost. When they embraced it was an affirmation that existence could be continued invisibly, that one could not imagine everything that might befall a neighbor. Every one of them was part of a web of tensile cousinships, adulteries, parishes, friendships, districts. The relationships stretched backwards to the names on gravestones, forward into putative births, and laterally into the remote distance. I thought: This is how the island makes itself the world; complexity is its signature; without it no one could live here; it would become like the empty islands of home, places where life had become too simple. This was the mirror of our island. There was never an undisclosed action, never an empty gesture, no secret.

Somewhere my father was brooding, waiting. In his island paradise at long last. Death too. That gentleman was patient. He waited for the next comer in his best suit. But not for me this time. Fathers do not live forever. We wait our turn, but they go first.

4

My father's new wife came. She was a delicate, courteous young woman. She called me *cara grazia*, delighted that I could speak her language, however badly. At first I thought, a little resentfully, that she was punning on my name. I had forgotten that grace and gratitude are linked by a common root. She dressed in dark neat clothes, her hair cut close to her head. She looked like a bundle of self-composure in a tight package. I had noticed before that Italian women, growing up in a chauvinist society, learned to be either docile or assertive. She spoke English in a limited way. She fed me olives and cool wine. She had heard about my trouble. These matters were so difficult. She hoped everything would be for the best. When I said something long and important about marriage she asked to have it translated. My father, I noticed, spoke in two tenses, the present and the recent past. A lazy grammarian. I could have translated as well myself. He did not look at me. Later, when he had gone to bed, she asked me if I had said something to upset him, he was sad, he was very sad. And angry, too. The Italian word for angry is *arrabbiato*. People think it has something to do with intemperate Arabs, but derives in fact from the Latin for *rabid* or *raving*. We saw the light come on in their room, we saw him close the shutters. I said we had disagreed about the past. She shook her pretty head. *Il passato*, she said. She made a puffing sound with her lips and a small explosive gesture with her fingers. It meant the past was gone. Young people can strike such poses. I saw its plume blowing away through the lemon grove. She made it sound so easy. I loved her for it. But I knew the ash would settle in the shadows. It would be there to mark us when we had forgotten it.

My sister came the next day.

My father didn't want to—he wasn't feeling well, he said—so I met her from the ferry and drove her to the house.

Where's Daddy?

I don't know, he said to collect you.

He always meets me.

Well, not today.

So she had been here before. Her hair seemed blacker. She had my mother's eyes, black as jet. In the sunshine she had the simplicity of a statue. She was wearing an Armani dress. She picked it up at an airport, she said, Paris, or maybe Rome. Her toenails were painted lime. They looked like one of her precious stones. Would you like a coffee? Yes please, would you mind boiling the milk?

Then came Bill. He was in tropical kit, he said. He wore his white linen suit. He had finally gotten around to making something with my father in it. He was bringing a documentary crew. They were staying at the Hotel Riviera and he thought he should stay with them but I knew it was because his researcher was there. This was not new. I almost divorced him once, for "playing away," as he liked to call it, but then my mother died and after that I got used to it. Habit, as someone said, is a great deadener.

He stayed with us.

He was excited, he said, about the prospect of finally doing something serious. The old man was a talker and the island would make a great setting. Radical finds peace in idyllic island, the vines, the trattoria, the narrow lanes, you know. He had a whole narrative of how my father's life had gone, from early political activism to a Zen-like composure in old age. The human interest was overwhelming. He was thinking about music and liked the idea of Bach cello suites, what did I think? They were deep, emotionally moving. He could talk crap like that for hours on end. But he knew his music, give him his due. He could hum the Bach Suite no. 1 in G, he said. This is the Courante—it'll be perfect. He hummed it now, waving his right hand to indicate the time. He sang in Saint Luke's Chelsea church choir, of all things. "Te Lucis Ante Terminum," rendered with gusto as if he believed in a plea to the creator to protect him through the night. Bill the Blessed and his angelic voice. He was probably fucking the sopranos.

Bald and fattening now, in bed he looked like a dead seal. His skin smelled slightly smoked. I told him he would have to stop wearing slim-fit shirts but he didn't listen to me. I told him he needed to get out of his car and walk. Precepts that might serve him well in the future.

Look at you, he said to me, you need to think body image.

This was how we expressed our hatred. In metaphor.

Where was the old man?

I said he was probably in his room. Something was eating him.

Don't tell me you upset him, I could do without family issues for god's sake.

He'll get over it, I said. Ask him if he thinks the Greens undermined the left because they gave capitalism a way to save face. Ask him if he thinks the Greens are the vegetarian bourgeoisie—that's what Mother used to call them. Ask him—

Oh, shut up, Grace, it's a bloody documentary, not a show trial.

Ask him if he thinks vegetables will save the world.

He chuckled at that. If he hadn't been such a hopeless shit

where women were concerned we might have made a go of it. If his ego hadn't needed so much feeding.

The air seemed to settle in my room, a viscous fluid slowly reducing in a hot pan so that the slightest stir left a visible wake. I slept and woke naked and covered in a slime of sweat, sore and slightly panicked, conscious of having passed a troubled hour or two but unable to remember anything other than the feeling of anxiety. In other circumstances I might have called it desire or fear. I took a cool shower. Afterwards the water dried on my skin. The silence of the big hot house. A feeling of fullness, secrecy, intensity, mourning. There were moments, instants really, when I thought someone was about to cry. It might have been me. I thought about Bill and the researcher going at it, the slime of sweat separating them, Bill's blubbery sex on her tiny frame. My sister probably knew. Father too. His pity. Their amusement. Bill can't keep it in his trousers.

I fell asleep eventually and woke at about four o'clock in the afternoon. Some of the brutal heat had gone.

There's no time like the present.

I heard snatches of conversation. Bill was there. He was with the camera crew in the garden setting up for the first interview. Sound, light, color, temperature. The shadow of the olives and the vines and the lemon grove. I heard him say that he was aiming for something biblical, a Caravaggio effect. He had no idea what he was talking about, of course, though it all seemed to be a common language. He could say it and they could make it happen. The terms, properly understood, made the world. The interview would be tomorrow, the morning of my father's birthday. Bill sometimes talked in terms of restoring my father's reputation, but he was talking about his own.

The geckos were still as stones. The cicadas called. There was no birdsong in the sun. There's no time like the present.

Across the way the old woman moved through the shade with her hoe and her can. There was a chair by the lemon tree and the ground looked like dust. There was a gecko on her wall, though you would think he was a stone unless you looked long at him. He was perched on the edge as though he were preparing to jump. Goodbye, cruel world.

I doubt the geckos think much of the world. They have all the appearance of cynics.

In the early evening I swam to clear my head. I needed to shake the heat from my heart. Swimming made me feel brave. It would give me the courage, I thought. Even from far out I could hear the brassy racket of the cicadas. It might have been time ringing in my ears. I swam out farther than the boats. Out to where I could feel the current of the Tyrrhenian Sea sweep around the headland taking me south towards Africa. Out in the deep sea you take a larger view of things. Continents come to mind, rivers of ocean, rivers of wind. I saw the broken lines of the island, the old volcanic ridges. I saw that there was an islet at one end joined to the rest by a bridge. And at the other was a walled village. I remembered my father saying the name—Terramurata. I saw the fire and ash of a million years frozen in time, the island thrust from the earth, the great maw and the smoke and the bubbling stone. Out I went. I saw my father's house, high up on the spine of the island, and someone standing outside. Could he see me? I recognized his shape, and, now that I was looking from a distance and could see only the shape of him, I saw that he had developed a stoop. Did he pity me? Poor Grace is married to Bill who can't keep it in his trousers, he doesn't even make a secret of it anymore.

There's no time like the present.

I swam back.

Out of my world.

I wore my bikini and a fine muslin shirt. I was long and straight and fit still.

I sent Bill a text. It was the least I could do. Fair warning. I met him in the garden of the Hotel Riviera. There was bougainvillea and a few waxy petals of gardenia. That dense, almost unbreathable air they make. You could drown in the scent of gardenia. Somewhere above us in a hot little room the researcher was rearranging her face. Putting her makeup on. A little bitch. They were all little.

I told him there in the garden. It was over.

He put his back to the balustrade and folded his arms. I knew Bill. I had studied his moods for years. I sensed a crisis. Something had unblocked in him. I prepared myself.

He said nothing for a time. Then very calmly he said: You knew I'd be like him.

He took me by surprise. First I wondered who he meant. Then I wondered if he was right.

He said: I knew that was why you married me. From the beginning. What does your lot call it? The Oedipus complex? Isn't there a cure for that yet? In fact, can you cure anything at all?

He laughed loudly. It was an unsettling, artificial sound.

But I'm the soul of discretion, he said. Don't think I'll mention it. To your fucked-up family. Mum's the word.

I tried to match his calm.

I want a divorce.

And you're welcome to it.

That's it, then.

What's all the fuss about? You could have said it anywhere. You could have sent me a fucking solicitor's letter.

There's no time like the present.

He pointed at me. Now I saw that his hand was shaking. Anger. Careful, Bill, anger will kill you. His father died of a stroke at fifty-seven. And now that I looked more closely at him I saw that he was sweating. His breathing was shallow. Bill was afraid of me. I knew what would come next.

Look at you, he said, you're like a stick insect. You're sick. If you'd seen a doctor years ago we wouldn't be like this now. You're completely fucking mad. You probably thought, I'll bring him out to this fucking shit-heap island complete with BBC fucking film crew and then I'll ruin his fucking film. Do you know how much setting this up cost? Do you have any idea what will happen to me if I don't pull it off? On second thought, of course you do. It was all part of your calculations, wasn't it? This is your revenge.

You should see yourself, Bill. You're shaking like a leaf. I thought you'd take this like a man.

Fuck you. Your whole family is screwed up. You picked the right profession. You're the worst of them all. All these years I've put up with your nerves and your fucking obsessions and your moods.

And so on. It was a brutal affair but I knew what I was doing. We were wrestlers but I was the only one with my feet on the ground. I had the strength of endings, of finality, of decision.

That's it, Bill, it's all over and done.

Then I said, Be on your best behavior at the birthday party tomorrow night, Bill. I promise you a treat.

He stared at me.

What are you up to now?

All the next day I stayed away. I wandered the island roads as far as they would take me. Bill hadn't come back.

The late afternoon bus was the pleasure of bodies, of crowding into an already crowded space, of hanging from a strap and feeling myself pushed this way and that by the contrapuntal sway, the press of people; the pleasure of smiling, the chatter, the music of happening. There was a space beneath my skin that wanted compression, that felt the absence of another body. Ghostly figures of lovers and children, half memory, half possibility; there was, at times, a fluttering that terrified me. I was thinking of severance and rupture and letting go. I was thinking of falling and jumping. I was thinking that this was the last time.

I felt emptied and filled by this crazy music, this cantata of community, of being together.

I felt I could face anything.

When I got home I found that Bill's clothes and laptop were gone. Where to? Wherever the little researcher was.

5

At my father's birthday dinner I sat with her. She had the body of a child and the eyes of a hungry dog. My father sat at the head of the table with Serena at his right hand and my sister at his left.

Bill was getting his film after all. Or calling my bluff.

He and the crew moved around the table, surveying us through the one good eye of the camera. When they came to me I waved. Hello, Bill, lovely to see you. Mosquitoes swarmed in the glare of the lighting—Bill had been experimenting with his Caravaggio effect. Before we sat down to eat we had all been given our instructions and now our skin glistened with DEET. It's a hundred percent effective, Bill said. He did not want the scene interrupted by people slapping insects or scratching. What he was hoping for, he said, was a biblical solemnity and a twenty-first-century joie de vivre. Even my father thought this was crap. Oh, Bill, he said, you do talk the talk, don't you? He seemed relaxed. The paterfamilias, the successful man among his adoring family.

The dinner was catered by Hotel Riviera, my father told us. Everything we would eat was local. He made a little speech, standing at the head of the table, Serena gazing up at him. Even the wine was from the next island where the *biancolella* vines grew, an ancient local stock, a wine that had to be enjoyed while young. I tipped my glass to Bill—Touché, I said, we had it for our honeymoon. People around me smiled.

The people who did the cooking, my father said, were neighbors, islanders all.

We were to feel virtuous because of all this. Never mind that his royalties alone would have bought half the island. We were to feel we were making a contribution. That this humble repast would make a difference to the world we had abused. In his heyday he was good at this. You were excoriated and affirmed at the same time.

We had fried flowers and little fish and mussels marinated in lemon and little parcels of cheese. Then we had a risotto bianco. Then we had chicken. The food was superb. No one can do a banquet like the Italians.

Anyone who had walked down through the grapes and the lemon trees might have met these fellows, he said, indicating the chicken and olive *secondi*. They lived in this very garden until their death and a very good time they had of it too.

He took pleasure in the reactions of the camera crew, their protests. We can't eat them now! But they did.

Bottles of young wine went round and round and afterwards there was grappa and Amaro Averna and Fernet-Branca. People took photographs. It was one of those perfect evenings. Father talked in a contrived way about the intensity of small, how the world needed it, how thinking big meant thinking energy, how rapacious capitalism had done for the world. He talked about Marx and Adam Smith and about low-energy, high-intensity production. About the greed of the corporation making water, earth, and air into commodities to be exploited. About power and discourse and multitude. I recognized the language and ideas from writers I was reading myself. I was surprised that in all this time he had been thinking and reading, but there was also regret—that it was all too late, that he thought he had made his mark and it was the wrong mark. Or that time had erased it.

Once, he said, we thought we could invent a new politics, but of course the old problems were still there and they had their politics too.

It was the lesson or the gospel or whatever it is they read. The dead air of a church service had settled on us. If there had been incense I would not have been surprised. All this solemnity. I wanted to say that feminism had done more to change the world than anything they could imagine. But there were other things I had to say.

His next lesson was, We missed our revolution.

First I almost laughed aloud, then I coughed loudly, the sound ending in a splutter. It may have been a bit theatrical, but I was conscious of the cameras. I heard Bill swearing somewhere outside the rim of light. I stood up.

I said I would like to take the opportunity to tell them that Bill and I were to be divorced. It might seem strange to say it here, I said, but since we were all gathered here together, breaking bread, as it were, all the people concerned—I raised my wineglass first to the shadows where Bill was recording the moment, then to the researcher, then to my father—I was happy to be able to tell everyone at the same time. And to have it recorded for posterity.

My father said congratulations with as much irony as he could muster considering I had shattered the air of solemnity with this trivial revelation. But I saw him glance at the little researcher.

Serena had to have the divorce business translated before she would believe I could say it here in public. I waited. It sounded sweeter and truer in Italian. It sounded like poetry. Then she cried. She may have been one of those people who believed in marriage despite the evidence, despite being an installation artist from the left-wing city of Genoa, where, possibly, installation artists are regarded as real artists and not funny architects. Then I proposed a toast for my father's birthday. I wished him long life and happiness in his island paradise. The glass I raised was half full of the blackness of Fernet. Everyone blithely echoed my words. Irony glistening like broken crystal in the soft night. Then I recited a poem for him, or at least a stanza and a line. It was Sylvia Plath:

> *So I never could tell where you*
> *Put your foot, your root,*
> *I never could talk to you.*
> *The tongue stuck in my jaw.*
>
> *It stuck in a barb wire snare.*

They didn't do toasts like that in the BBC.

My father stared at me. Serena wanted a translation. He put out his hand to her, but it was a gesture of control. She stopped.

I held my glass towards him again. I was conscious of the film moving frame by frame past the lens. I guessed that Bill would want this piece of drama preserved, whatever about the divorce announcement. It would make riveting television, a reality show that was real. We're using film stock, he said, for that special atmosphere. You can't catch it any other way. Bill's old-fashioned virtues. I'll say this, he made some pretty documentaries.

You are a guest at my table, my father said.

He pointed at me. He tried to say something else, the words stuttering like a clockwork gone wrong. I never heard what they were. Serena had her hand on his arm. A comfort or a restraint? What do you say now, Daddy? What do you say now? He shook her hand off. Serena looked up at him. She was frightened. Some of us held glass, some did not, according to our place in the ancient pledge.

I may have been a little drunk. In my small frame even a little alcohol is enough.

Stop it, my sister shouted. She plucked at my clothes.

Lights, camera, action, I said. I may have waved my glass. Something gleamed in the light that might have been glass or liquid. This is better than Caravaggio, Bill, I said, The Death of the Family Newman, bestseller's daughter fucks up the party.

Christ, my father said, the film, for Christ's sake, Bill, stop it.

I had his attention now. For the first time in my life.

But Bill said nothing. Good old Bill. The consummate professional. This is my parting gift to you, Bill.

You kept it all under wraps, I said to my father, you buttoned us down, you were the master of ceremonies. You used us, you stole our island. You used our lives to make money. You're a charlatan. Here's to you, the great liar, the denier, the hider, here's to the redistribution of guilt to each according to his need. You made me lie to the coroner when my sister Em died. And you made me swear to it. You wrecked my mother's mind. All these years I blamed myself. Years and years of guilt. You ruined our lives. You could have saved her, but you didn't. If you loved her she would never have died. And Em would never have died. She'd be here at this table now, drinking to your health, Emily my sister.

Some obstacle in my throat rising and falling like a cork on a wave. I was crying. I needed to master it. I took a deep breath.

Here's what I want to tell you, Tom, on your seventieth birthday: I blame you. We all do.

I knew I was crying. I felt as if my brain were breaking down. Those words stuttered out of me. I was disintegrating. I was shaking myself apart.

There was no glasshouse, I said.

I think I shouted it. The silence was instant. Only two of us knew what it meant. Everyone else held their breath.

He looked at me for what seemed like a long time. I could see he was trying to remember. Then he looked away and looked back again. There was something blind in the second look.

It was you, he said. You stole the book.

Yes.

Now he was looking down at his lap. His head was trembling, an infinitely small but definite vibration. Old age has laid her hand upon me. Bill and his camera moved a little closer.

It would have been my best book, he said. A certain bestseller.

It was a book of lies.

He looked at me again and this time there was an appeal in it. I could do it now, at his weakest moment, destroy him as simply as breaking a bird's neck. I said nothing.

What did you do with it?

I put it in a bin at Waterloo.

Did you read it?

No. A few pages, no more.

God.

I knew what it was about, I said. I knew the ending.

His lips and the tip of his nose were white. His breathing was fast. He was sitting very straight.

You're a vicious little bitch, he said. A sinister little bitch. Jesus Christ.

He stood up awkwardly and stumbled and sat down again.

No more, Serena said, please, *basta*!

She put her arms around him but she was looking at me.

She was a delicate woman. Those ideal forms that Italy makes. Her dark eyebrows were charcoal lines on a face that was shaped for pity. Her lips full as cherries. Her perfect breasts. Her boy's hips. Everyone at the table was in love with her. When she admonished me I sat down.

My sister comforted her. She held her hand. No one held mine. No one looked at me. I let the evening go. Darkness got past the lights. It flooded the lemon trees and fireflies appeared.

6

Bill didn't come home. I wasn't surprised. I heard he was living with someone in Putney. I heard she worked for a fashion magazine. His next real manifestation was a Form D10: the petitioner therefore prays that the said marriage may be dissolved, etc., etc. He cited unreasonable behavior as the grounds for divorce. It seemed a bizarre choice to me, but my solicitor assured me it would make no difference. I went out to dinner to celebrate, but afterwards, coming home on the busy bus, I felt my life had somehow darkened, that a shade had fallen—or perhaps a filter that eliminated certain characteristics of the light. For a long time there was something tenebrous even about morning, and nights were bleak. We are to think that the departure of someone who has been part of our psyche, no matter what role they played, must inevitably be felt as loss, and I suppose I was bereft in some way, even if at the conscious level I was happy to be rid of him. Anyway, I survived.

My sister had elected herself as my support. I found it strange that divorce had precipitated me into the role of patient or victim. Until now I had imagined myself as the strong one, my sister the waif, the underdog.

She told me that my father forgave me. It made me angry and at the same time ashamed. What did he mean by forgiveness? And for what? Did he understand anything?

He says he's going to write to you, she said.

Tell him I won't read it.

I won't do your dirty work, Grace.

I shrugged. It's not his place to forgive anyone.

She looked at me. You know, for a clinical psychologist you really haven't a clue.

I grinned at her.

I'm on edge a bit, I said. I keep seeing Bill in crowds. It's ridiculous. It's like a girl in love. I see him from the bus. I see him ahead of me on escalators, getting off the tube. I'm seeing more of the bastard than I did when we were married. Is there an epidemic of obesity in London?

She reached across and held my hand. Just read the letter, she said. Promise.

Touch undoes us always. I was screwed tight and now I was spiraling into tears. I looked away. She squeezed my hand again. My sister comforting me. It felt so strange.

It's all right, Grace, she said.

In time I turned back.

I saw a shipwreck once. In Cornwall or Devon, or at least I saw the wrecked ship. A small coaster had mistaken its place at the entrance to a harbor. Finding the error, it had attempted to turn, and in the process, while the engines were being put into reverse but the ship was still carrying its way, it ran onto a sandstone outcrop. That was a night of fog. Then came a series of southwesterly gales that lasted almost three weeks. I watched from a distance as the ship was first broken in two, the head tipped forward into deeper water, and finally battered with astonishing force until the original structure had all but disappeared. At the end of it, the stern section resembled nothing but a stamped-on drink can.

I thought often about the mistakes the captain had made: how in the fog he had missed the lighthouse, how too late he had seen it and begun the fatal turn. From the technical point of view, had the maneuver, ill-chosen or not, been executed correctly? The sequence only seems inexorable in retrospect. In reality every moment is infinite and capable of infinite possibility. How many of the possibilities would have resulted in the same outcome? I thought of my mother, the way she held Em between her legs when she was sitting, one arm wrapped around her chest, or caressing her hair.

The first letter arrived on a Monday morning. The letters came every two or three days. Some were long like the first, some short. They were mostly reminiscences, and more than once I wondered if they were excerpts from some new memoir he was writing, or rough drafts. At first I did not reply. Five letters came before I wrote a word. I responded because he asked me if I wanted him to continue. I have always been capable of great coldness. It's what makes me a good psychologist. And a bad lover. I said that the letters were clearly fulfilling some need in him. He should continue until that need had been satisfied. None came that week, nor the next. I regretted my reply almost as soon as I put the letter in the post. As the days dragged on I began to think about asking my sister. In the end I phoned her up. She didn't know I had been getting letters. She may have been jealous. Twice I picked up the phone to call him. I wanted to apologize. I wanted to say I regretted everything. But then a new letter came. It was a day of stupefying downpours. The streets clattered with rain. The noise of cars, their wheels spewing water like broken pipes. People rushing past under umbrellas, wearing those transparent plastic coats and ponchos. Tourists, swamped by London. He was telling me that he was dying. Or just that he was getting old. I was disturbed, as much by my own sudden apprehension as by the possibility of losing him. A door opened onto my own mortality. While our parents live we imagine lights between ourselves and the great gloaming. And I was suddenly conscious of the waste—all those years that I hated him. I called my sister and arranged to meet her in Kettner's. It was her choice. It was founded by a chef of Napoleon's. It was a place that was conscious of some faded belle epoque that never quite happened.

He's not dying, she said. He's as strong as an ox.

But he wrote: I feel my time is coming to an end, the weather is closing in. And he wants me to write a book. About the family.

Really? How extraordinary.

On the last page of the letter he asked me to write the book that I had destroyed. *Write it your own way, you know the story.*

Grace, I told you, he forgave you.

He's still trying to control his legacy.

He told you to write it your own way.

But he knows I can't do that. There will always be his voice in my head.

You're so full of bullshit, Grace. Everything is psychology. Do you ever have a simple unmediated reaction to anything human? One of the reasons I like geology is because a stone is a stone, its future is much the same as its past, it doesn't require analysis except in relation to time. Humans can be like that too, you know? You can just be.

I know.

What do you know?

I know I can't do that.

For God's sake!

I walked my sister to a taxi under my umbrella. Our legs were wet. The leather of my shoes turned from tan to black. As soon as a cab stopped the rain stopped too and almost immediately Romilly Street, shabby Soho, lit up like some kind of ice sculpture on a hot day. As she stood with the taxi door open we both looked up and laughed. She gave me a quick hug and I handed her the Marks and Spencer's bag.

What's this?

It's his book. Send it to him.

You never destroyed it?

No. I kept it. It's been in a drawer in my bedroom all this time. I'm looking forward to being able to use the drawer again. He can finish it now.

I could see she was shocked.

The meter is running, I said.

All this time, she said. Then she got in and closed the door. I saw her put the bag on the seat beside her and tell the driver where she was going.

Two weeks later I came home from work to find a parcel from Italy containing the same olive-green Marks and Spencer bag and the same weight of paper. There was no letter. The pages looked undisturbed. I didn't know what to do.

7

We scattered his ashes on the island. It was his will. The day was blustery. A cold wind from Greenland or somewhere else to the northwest had cleared the air. There were occasional heavy showers and strong gales, but you could see forever. The rocks were as clean as monuments, their striae and strata marked out like pencil strokes. We went out on Johnny Casey's fishing boat from Rally Pier. It was there waiting, tied to the wall, when we arrived. And while we traveled we watched the seas breaking outside the harbor. My father in the wheelhouse in a small wooden box of cedar; inside there would be a screw-cap plastic jar and the contents would be him. We come down to so little. The shakings of a tea caddy, with stray fragments of bone. After the fire we are not even clay.

The trawler landed us at the pier under the old tower. My sister and I looked at the place where I found Em. We caught each other's eye. Here in the lee of the island the water was the same translucent green and I could see the stones at the bottom and the sea's long hair, kelp and bladder-wrack, lying out in lines with the current. We made our way along the old road until the place where it had fallen into the sea and then we went up into the fields. I saw again the Jurassic fronds of the bracken, the quivering webs. Seabirds called. The sea thundered onto the shore and the shore stood its ground and drove it back. But there were losses. Each time something died.

The house was still dry. The roof had not fallen in. There was glass in the windows. There was some kindling by the fire. An ash block was a nest of woodlice. They had hollowed it out. My sister took it outside and shook them out. Then we burned it. The flame warmed us even though the room slowly filled with smoke.

Suddenly, inexplicably, I was happy. I found two glasses. I had brought a naggin of whiskey. I cleaned the glasses with my shirttail and poured some for each of us. The taste of flame. Here's to you, my father, my lost father, my past, my sister Em. We drank it back. Whiskey always brings tears to my eyes.

The night I returned to London I went into the bedroom. I opened the bottom drawer of my dressing table. It didn't open easily. I got his book out of the bag and took it to my desk, a solid block of typescript. Time had finished it. I knew the ending now.

Opening the drawer was like drawing a deep breath.

I could begin again.

I could build something with that block. I sat down and opened my laptop. I started a new document. I typed my first words. I already knew what they would be. It was as if I had been composing them for years, but in truth they came to me on the island, that day after we had opened the twist-cap a second time, then offered his ashes to the wind and the stony beach. It was sheltered there and the small waves made no sound we could hear. He blew away onto the tide and we put the heavier parts into the heather at the field's edge. If I could have prayed I would have, but my mother neglected to teach us about eternity.

I would write it for Em, for the life she never knew, the loves she never experienced. I would write her future.

A long time ago I had two sisters and we lived on an island. There was me and Jeannie and Em. They called me Grace, but I have never had much of that. I was an awkward child. I still am all these years later. Our house had two doors, one to the south, one to the north. Its garden looked towards the setting sun.

The moon over the city. The ragtag roofs of east London, its merry gables and hips and saws and skillions and mansards and pavilions. Far below, an ambulance was trying to edge between two badly parked cars. Its lights were winding silently. Down the street a red man changed to a green one but no one was there to make the crossing. There were pools on the road. There is a game for every eventuality. Tomorrow is a spinning coin, heads or tails, nobody knows which is better. I turned the radio on. It was the shipping forecast. They were giving Lundy, Fastnet, southwesterly six to gale eight, occasionally severe gale nine at first. I don't know why it made me cry. I thought of the wind driving over the island and children sheltering in their beds, darkness hammering on the roof. Life blows through like a hurricane stripping everything from us, leaves from a tree, old washing from a clothesline, illusions, dreams, affections, hope. The wind in the walls said, Lonesome child, go away, go home, childhood is a shadow on the floor. I turned but my mother was not there. I saw a crow breaking a mussel on a stone. He had the shell trapped under his claw. Water rushed in and out, sweeping the ground from under me, drawing me on a long cable, its windlass far away.

ACKNOWLEDGMENTS

I wish to express my gratitude to The Bogliasco Foundation/Fondazione Bogliasco, which provided me with time to research and write the Italian stories in this book. Versions of the opening story, "Grace's Day," were first published in the *Prairie Schooner* and won the Virginia Faulkner Award and subsequently appeared in English in *Lost Between* (New Island Books) and in Italian in *Tra Una Vita e L'Altra* (Guanda). The story "The Mountain Road" first appeared in *Granta* magazine and was subsequently published in my collection *Hearing Voices, Seeing Things* (Doire Press).